AFTERNOON OF THE ELVES

 *A Richard Jackson Book*

ALSO BY THE AUTHOR

The Dancing Cats of Applesap

Sirens and Spies

The Great Dimpole Oak

AFTERNOON of the ELVES

ʞ ʞ ʞ ʞ ʞ ʞ

Janet Taylor Lisle

Orchard Books · New York

A division of Franklin Watts, Inc.

Orchard Books, a division of Franklin Watts, Inc.
387 Park Avenue South
New York, NY 10016

Manufactured in the United States of America
Book design by Mina Greenstein
The text of this book is set in 12 pt. Janson
10 9 8 7 6 5 4 3 2 1

Library of Congress Cataloging-in-Publication Data
Lisle, Janet Taylor.
Afternoon of the elves / Janet Taylor Lisle. p. cm.
Summary: As Hillary works in the miniature village, allegedly
built by elves, in Sara-Kate's backyard, she becomes more and
more curious about Sara-Kate's real life inside her big, gloomy
house with her mysterious, silent mother.
ISBN 0-531-05837-9.   ISBN 0-531-08437-X (lib. bdg.)
I. Title.
PZ7.L6912Af 1989 [Fic]—dc19 88-35099 CIP AC

 For Elizabeth
a friend to elves

One ✂

The afternoon Hillary first saw the elf village, she couldn't believe her eyes.

"Are you sure it isn't mice?" she asked Sara-Kate, who stood beside her, thin and nervous. "The houses are small enough for mice."

"No, it isn't," Sara-Kate said. "Mice don't make villages in people's backyards."

Hillary got down on her hands and knees to look more closely. She counted the tiny houses. There were nine, each made of sticks bound delicately together with bits of string and wire.

"And there's a well," she whispered, "with a bucket that winds down on a string to pull the water out."

"Not a bucket. A bottlecap!" snorted Sara-Kate, twitching her long, shaggy hair away from her face. She was eleven, two years older than Hillary, and she had never spoken to the younger girl before. She had hardly looked at her before.

"Can I try drawing some water?" Hillary asked.

Sara-Kate said, "No."

The roofs of the houses were maple leaves attached to the sticks at jaunty angles. And because it was autumn, the leaves were lovely colors, orange-red, reddish-orange, deep yellow. Each house had a small yard in front neatly bordered with stones that appeared to have come from the driveway.

"They used the leaves dropping off those trees over there," Hillary said.

Sara-Kate shrugged. "Why not? The leaves make the houses pretty."

"How did they get these stones all the way over here?" Hillary asked.

"Elves are strong," Sara-Kate said. "And magic."

Hillary looked at her suspiciously then. It wasn't that she didn't believe so much as that she couldn't right away put Sara-Kate on the side of magic. There never had been one pretty thing about her. Nothing soft or mysterious. Her face was narrow and ended in a sharp chin, and her eyes were small and hard as bullets. They were such little eyes, and set so deeply in her head, that the impression she gave was of a gaunt, fierce bird, a rather untidy bird if one took her clothes into consideration. They hung on her frame, an assortment of ill-fitting, wrinkly garments. ("Doesn't she care how she looks?" a new girl at school had inquired just this fall, giving every child within earshot the chance to whirl around and shout, "No!")

Least magical of all, Sara-Kate Connolly wore boots that were exactly like the work boots worn by men in gas stations.

"Black and greasy," Hillary's friend Jane Webster said.

"She found them at the dump," Alison Mancini whispered.

"No she didn't. Alison, that's terrible!"

Normally, fourth graders were too sh[y] comment on students in higher grades. But [Sara-] Kate had been held back in school that year. She was taking the fifth grade all over again, which made her a curiosity.

"Can you tell me where you found those amazing boots? I've just got to get some exactly like them," Jane said to her one day, wearing a look of such innocence that for a second nobody thought to laugh.

In the middle of Sara-Kate's backyard, Hillary recalled the sound of that laughter while she stared at Sara-Kate's boots. Then she glanced up at Sara-Kate's face.

"Why does it have to be elves? Why couldn't it be birds or chipmunks or some animal we've never heard of? Or maybe some person made these houses," Hillary said, a sly tone in her voice. She got off her knees and stood up beside the older girl. "We are the same height!" she announced in surprise.

They were almost the same except for Sara-Kate's thinness. Hillary was sturdily built and stood on wide feet.

"In fact, I'm even a little taller!" Hillary exclaimed, rising up a bit on her toes and looking down.

Sara-Kate stepped away from her quickly. She folded her arms across her chest and beamed her small, hard eyes straight into Hillary's wide ones.

"Look," she said. "I didn't have to invite you over

· 3

here today and I didn't have to show you this. I thought you might like to see an elf village for a change. If you don't believe it's elves, that's your problem. I *know* it's elves."

So, there they were: elves—a whole village of them living down in Sara-Kate's junky, overgrown backyard that was itself in back of Sara-Kate's broken-down house with the paint peeling off. Sara-Kate's yard was not the place Hillary would have picked to build a village if she were an elf. Where there weren't thistles and weeds there was mud, and in the mud, broken glass and wire and pieces of rope. There were old black tires and rusty parts of car engines and a washing machine turned over on its side. Carpets of poison ivy grew under the trees and among the bushes. Nobody ever played in Sara-Kate's backyard. But then, as Sara-Kate would have said, nobody had ever been invited to play in her backyard. Except Hillary, that is, on that first afternoon of the elves.

"Sara-Kate Connolly thinks she's got elves," Hillary told her mother when she came home, rather late, from looking at the village. The yards of the two families backed up to each other, a source of irritation to Hillary's father, who believed that property should be kept up to standard. But who could he complain to? Sara-Kate's father did not live there anymore. ("He's away on a trip," Sara-Kate always said.) And Sara-Kate's mother didn't care about yards. She hardly ever went outside. She kept the

4 ·

shades of the house drawn down tight, even in summer.

"Elves?" Mrs. Lenox repeated.

"They're living in her backyard," Hillary said. "They have little houses and a well. I said it must be something else but Sara-Kate is sure it's elves. It couldn't be, could it?"

"I don't like you playing in that yard," Hillary's mother told her. "It's not a safe place for children. If you want to see Sara-Kate, invite her over here."

"Sara-Kate won't come over here. She never goes to other people's houses. And she never invites anyone to her house," Hillary added significantly. She tried to flick her hair over her shoulder the way Sara-Kate had done it that afternoon. But the sides were too short and refused to stay back.

"It seems that Sara-Kate is beginning to change her mind about invitations," Mrs. Lenox said then, with an unhappy bend in the corners of her mouth.

But how could Hillary invite Sara-Kate to play? And play with what? The elves were not in Hillary's backyard, which was neat and well-tended, with an apple tree to climb and a round garden filled with autumn flowers. Hillary's father had bought a stone birdbath at a garden shop and placed it on a small mound at the center of the garden. He'd planted ivy on the mound and trained it to grow up the birdbath's fluted stem. Birds came from all over the neighborhood to swim there, and even squirrels and chipmunks dashed through for a dip. The birdbath made the garden beautiful.

"Now it's a real garden," Hillary's father had said proudly, and, until that afternoon, Hillary had agreed. She had thought it was among the most perfect gardens on earth.

Sara-Kate's elves began to change things almost immediately, however. Not that Hillary really believed in them. No, she didn't. Why should she? Sara-Kate was not her friend. But, even without being believed, magic can begin to change things. It moves invisibly through the air, dissolving the usual ways of seeing, allowing new ways to creep in, secretly, quietly, like a stray cat sliding through bushes.

"Sara-Kate says elves don't like being out in the open," Hillary remarked that evening as she and her father strolled across their garden's well-mowed lawn. She found herself examining the birdbath with new, critical eyes.

"She says they need weeds and bushes to hide under, and bottlecaps and string lying around to make their wells."

Mr. Lenox didn't answer. He had bent over to fix a piece of ivy that had come free from the birdbath.

"And stones on their driveways," Hillary added, turning to gaze at her own driveway, which was tarred down smooth and flat.

She turned toward Sara-Kate's house next. Its dark form loomed behind the hedge at the bottom of the yard. Though evening had come, no light showed in any of the windows.

Now that Hillary thought about it, she could not remember ever seeing many lights down there. Gray and expressionless was how the house generally appeared. What could Sara-Kate and her mother be doing inside? Hillary wondered, and, for a moment, she had a rather grim vision of two shapes sitting motionless at a table in the dark.

Then she remembered the shades. Mrs. Connolly's shades must be drawn so tightly that not a ray of light could escape. Behind them, Sara-Kate was probably having dinner in the kitchen, or she was doing her homework.

"What happened at school today?" her mother would be asking her. Or, "Please don't talk with your mouth full!"

Hillary imagined Sara-Kate Connolly frowning after this remark. She felt sure that Sara-Kate was too old to be reminded of her manners. Too old and too tough. Not really the kind of person to have elves in her backyard, Hillary thought.

"I'm going inside!" Hillary's father's voice sounded from across the lawn. The rest of him was swallowed up by dark.

"Wait for me. Wait!" Hillary cried. She didn't want to be left behind. Night had fallen so quickly, like a great black curtain on a stage. In a minute she might have been quite frightened except that suddenly, through the garden, the twinkling lights of the fireflies burst forth. It was as if the little bugs had waited all day for this moment to leap out of hiding. Or had they been there all along, blinking steadily but invisibly in the daylight? Hillary paused and looked about.

"Hillary! Where are you?"

"Coming," she called, and turned to run in. A gust of wind slid across her cheek. Like lanterns in the grip of magic hands, the tiny lights flickered over the lawn.

TWO

Hillary dreamed about elves during the night. By morning it was clear that the magic of Sara-Kate's elves must be real, for while Hillary slept, it crept, mysterious and cat-like as ever, out of the Connollys' backyard, up the hill and through the half-opened window of Hillary's bedroom. There she woke beneath its spell shortly after dawn and immediately was seized by a mad desire to run down to Sara-Kate's yard in her nightgown.

But what would Sara-Kate have thought? And suppose the elves were not such early risers? Hillary imagined them surprised in their beds, leaping for cover as her giant bare feet thudded over the ground toward the fragile village. She made herself dress for school instead. She gathered her school books with unusual attention to orderliness and went downstairs to the kitchen. Hillary was determined to visit the elf village again soon, that very afternoon if Sara-Kate would have her. In the meantime, she ate a large breakfast of pancakes and milk, walked to school four blocks away, and spoke privately to Jane Webster and Alison Mancini about what she had seen in the Connollys' yard.

"Elves!" shrieked Jane and Alison together.

They were standing in front of their lockers taking

off their denim jackets, which were identical, each with silver stars sewn on the shoulders and down the front. Hillary was wearing the same jacket, too. Their mothers had bought them in the same store downtown even though they were rather expensive. It was such fun to dress alike, as if they were members of a select club.

"What kind of elves?" Alison asked suspiciously.

Hillary told them about the little yards. She described the stones bordering the yards and the neatness of it all.

"Are there gates?" Alison wanted to know.

"I don't think so," Hillary said.

"Are there chimneys? How about mailboxes?"

Hillary shook her head to both. "There's no furniture or anything inside. They're just, you know, little houses."

Alison shrugged. She and Jane looked at each other.

"I bet she made them herself," Jane said.

"Maybe she did," Hillary replied. "And maybe she didn't. You should come see."

"All right, we will," Alison said, pushing the sleeves of her sweater up her arms with two smart strokes. She was the best dressed of the three. Jane was brighter, though. Her mother was a lawyer. Why they had alighted upon baby-faced Hillary for the third in their group even Hillary didn't know. She was often awed by their sophisticated conversations.

"We'll come, but don't think we'll be fooled for a minute," Alison said.

Jane put on the sweet and innocent face that always meant something awful was coming. "I'd be interested to see if anything can live in that sickening backyard," she said to Hillary as the bell for class rang. "Besides Sara-Kate, that is."

She was not allowed to find out because Sara-Kate refused to have her. Sara-Kate refused to invite Alison either, though Hillary asked as nicely as possible. Jane and Alison waited out of sight in an empty classroom.

"But why?" Hillary begged. "You've got to let them come."

The thin girl shook her head and raised her voice slightly. "These elves are private people. They aren't for public display. You can come if you want, but not those two creeps."

"They're not creeps. We're friends," Hillary protested.

But Sara-Kate, who didn't have any friends, who spit at people when they made her mad and walked around all day in a pair of men's boots, only smiled faintly.

"Some friends!" she announced, in a voice that carried straight down the hall to Jane and Alison's furious ears.

"Sara-Kate Connolly is not a nice person," Alison said to the group when Hillary returned. "She gets in trouble a lot. Hillary should be careful of her."

Jane nodded. "Anyone can say she has an elf village in her backyard if she wants to. The point is, where are the elves? I bet Sara-Kate is the only person who ever sees them."

"Nobody sees them," Hillary said. "Not even Sara-Kate. They go away when they hear people coming. Elves are very private persons. Sara-Kate said they used to be seen in the old days, but not now because there are too many people around and they're frightened. Elves haven't been seen for over a hundred years."

"If these elves are so real, why doesn't Sara-Kate want us to come look?" Jane inquired, casting a shrewd glance at Alison.

"Because they're fake," Alison answered without waiting for Hillary to reply. "Just like Sara-Kate."

"She's definitely not a person you want to trust," Jane agreed. She lowered her voice and drew the friends closer. "Do you remember that new bike she was riding to school last spring? Do you remember how she boasted about it and said she had a job on a paper route? Have you noticed how she isn't riding it anymore this fall?"

Alison nodded.

"What happened?" Hillary asked.

"She stole it," Jane whispered. "From a store downtown. Everybody knows. The police came to Sara-Kate's house and she was arrested. Only, she gave the bike back so nothing happened. They're watching her, though, in case she steals something else."

Hillary was shocked. "How awful!"

For the rest of the day she kept away from Sara-Kate. When she walked home from school, she saw

12 ·

her thin shape in the distance and it looked dangerous suddenly. It looked like the shape of someone
who was bad, someone who lived in a bad house
and came from a bad family.

If magic had truly invaded Hillary's room, now
it slithered away again. It was gone by the time she
reached home that day, and Hillary was relieved.
She felt as if she had made a narrow escape and
laughed at herself for being so easily fooled. She
began to remember other incidents connected with
Sara-Kate Connolly. They were little things—a lost
pencil case, a series of small disappearances from the
art room, a mean note left in someone's desk. Taken
together, they added up to something larger in Hillary's mind.

"I do think it's best not to spend time down in
that yard," Mrs. Lenox said, approvingly, at dinner.
"Heaven knows what you might catch or step on."

Two days later, Hillary had put the elf village
almost completely out of her mind when Sara-Kate
appeared at her elbow in the hall at school. She
appeared so suddenly, and at such an odd time—all
the other fifth graders were at sports—that Hillary
jumped.

Sara-Kate leaned toward her and spoke in a high,
breathless voice.

"Where have you been? I thought you were coming again. The elves have built a playground. They
have a swimming pool and a Ferris wheel now." She
flung a string of hair over her shoulder and smiled

nervously. "You should come see," she told Hillary.

"A Ferris wheel!" In spite of herself, Hillary felt a jab of excitement. "How did they build that?"

"With Popsicle sticks and two bicycle wheels. It really goes around. The elves come out at night and play on it. Really and truly," said Sara-Kate, looking into Hillary's eyes. "I can tell it's been used in the morning."

Hillary glanced away, down at the floor, where she noticed that both of Sara-Kate's boots were newly speckled with mud. Her legs rose out of them, two raw, white stalks that disappeared under her skirt's ragged hem. She didn't seem to be wearing any socks at all. Half of Hillary was repelled. No one in the school was so badly dressed as Sara-Kate, or so mean and unhealthy-looking. And yet, another half was strangely tempted.

"Maybe I could come over this afternoon," she told the older girl. "Just for a minute, though. I've got a lot of things to do."

Sara-Kate's small eyes narrowed. "In that case, don't bother."

"I want to," Hillary said, "but my mother—"

"Who cares!" Sara-Kate interrupted. "Who cares about your stupid mother."

"She's afraid I'll catch poison ivy."

"Do I have poison ivy?" Sara-Kate extended one of her skinny arms for Hillary's inspection. "Is there one bit of poison ivy on me?"

Hillary shook her head. Sara-Kate's skin was pale,

but unmarked. Her nails were cut short and her hands were clean.

"You won't catch poison ivy, but don't bother to come anyway," Sara-Kate said. "These elves don't like a lot of people looking at their stuff. They aren't show-offs like most of the creeps around here."

"It isn't that," Hillary tried to say, but Sara-Kate had turned her back. She began to walk away, and Hillary could see from the stiffness in her shoulders and the line of her chin that she was hurt.

"Wait a minute!" she called. "Wait! I forgot to ask you something."

But it was too late. Sara-Kate had passed beyond the limits of reasonable conversation.

"I know what it is," she sneered over her shoulder, "and I'm not answering. Even if I told you you wouldn't believe me. You wouldn't, would you?" she shouted at Hillary, while other people in the hall stopped to stare at her: at her clothes and her boots and her hair falling over her face. "You just wouldn't, none of you!" she shrieked, losing control in a way most unlike her. She began to run and hop along the hall in the strangest fashion, with knotted fists and flying feet. Like an elf, Hillary thought. Sara-Kate's face had turned bright red. She looked exactly like a tiny, silly, cartoon elf trying to run away fast and getting nowhere.

"Creeps!" Sara-Kate screamed, with her boots drumming into the floor.

Along the corridor, groups of students moved carefully out of her way.

Three ✗

At a little past three o'clock on the same afternoon, Hillary went through the hedge into the Connollys' backyard. She sneaked through, looking first right, then left, but whether she was afraid of being seen by Mrs. Lenox, or by Sara-Kate on the other side, or by the elusive elves themselves, she didn't know. She felt sure that she should not have come at all. Sara-Kate was too strange. Her house was too shabby. Hillary should have stayed home, safe in her kitchen. She should have read a book or baked a cake with her mother. There were ten other things she might have done, but, by the thinnest thread of enchantment, the elf village was drawing her.

How did it do that? What was its magic? Hillary could not shut out pictures of the curious houses that crept into her head. She could not forget the leaf roofs. The little well appeared and disappeared, wavered and vanished in her imagination in a most maddening way, like Alice's Cheshire Cat. The Ferris wheel was the strongest lure. She could not quite visualize how it would look, and came out her back door in a sort of trance from trying so hard to see.

Hillary's enchantment did not extend to Sara-

Kate, however, and the closer she came to the Connollys' yard, the more she hoped that Sara-Kate would not be there. The voices of Jane and Alison came back to her. She heard their sensible warnings again, but softer now, muffled by some other power.

The boughs of the hemlock hedge presented Hillary with a thick, green curtain. Passing through, she was forced to raise her arms to protect her face, to close her eyes—and, for a moment, there was a frightening feeling of walking blind into a trap. But when she opened her eyes, only the Connollys' backyard came into view, as weedy and trash-strewn as ever. Away to the right, a figure slouched on a pile of wooden planks, looking more like the lone survivor of a wreck at sea than the violent, unpredictable girl it must be. Hillary shoved her hands into her pockets. She approached warily and had come within a few feet of the woodpile when Sara-Kate's head turned and her two tiny eyes flicked wide with surprise.

"You!" Sara-Kate exclaimed. Then she sprang to her feet, and whatever had been bowed or sad about her before vanished in an instant. She leapt off the pile of planks, landing exactly beside Hillary. Her boots made almost no sound hitting the ground. Sara-Kate gathered her long, straw-colored hair behind her head with a sweep of one hand and let it fall down her back. She grinned and hooked her thumbs into the waistband of her old skirt.

"Hi!" she said. "I thought you weren't coming."

"Well, I did," Hillary mumbled.

"The Ferris wheel's over there," Sara-Kate said, pointing.

They went to look right away. Hillary drew a deep breath. It was twice as big as she had expected, and constructed in such a complicated manner that one look told her it was the work of special hands. Two bicycle wheels without their rubber tires were suspended face to face above the ground on a metal rod that passed through the wheels' centers. The rod's tips rested on up-ended cinder blocks. The Popsicle sticks that Sara-Kate had mentioned were attached by strings to the wheels' outer rims and hung down horizontally to act as long seats. Numerous pieces of wire linked the spokes of the two wheels, so that when they turned, they turned as one and a marvelous pattern of wires and spokes was woven before the eye.

"How did it get here?" Hillary asked softly.

"It just was here, yesterday morning when I came out of the house," Sara-Kate replied, with such wonder in her own voice that Hillary had no doubt it was the truth. She looked at Sara-Kate with admiring eyes.

"I'm still not sure how the elves make it go," Sara-Kate went on. "I've gone over the whole thing and I can't find a motor anywhere. Probably they have some power or current that we don't know about. Naturally, we humans have to spin the wheel by hand."

She reached out as she spoke and spun the wheel

hard, transforming the wires and sticks into a series of gold and silver flickers.

"Now you try," she said to Hillary. She didn't mention her rage in the hall at school that morning. She treated Hillary respectfully, as if she were a special friend.

"It doesn't matter where you hold the wheel," Sara-Kate said in a most reasonable and helpful voice. "Just grab it anywhere and spin."

Hillary, who had never ridden on a Ferris wheel, leaned forward shyly and turned the wheel. It was very large, so large that it would have lifted a person far, far off the ground, she thought . . . if that person happened to be the size of an elf.

Hillary crouched beside the Ferris wheel. She made her eyes level with the highest seat and looked to see what an elf's view of the yard would be. There was the rusty white side of the washing machine rising through weeds like a mountain peak. There was the top of a tree stump appearing above the green jungle like the smoke stack of an ocean liner. The yard looked enormous from this vantage, and dense with greenery. In the distance, Sara-Kate's house towered over all, a rather frightening gray fortress.

"Have you ever wondered what it would feel like to be an elf?" Hillary asked Sara-Kate. "I mean, how would it feel to be so strange and little?"

Sara-Kate's eyes jumped to Hillary's face.

"What do you mean 'strange and little'?" she inquired sharply. "If you were an elf you wouldn't feel strange or little. You'd feel like a normal, healthy elf."

"Sorry," said Hillary, "I didn't mean—"

"Yes, you did," Sara-Kate interrupted. She pushed Hillary's hand away from the Ferris wheel and halted its spin with a single finger stabbed between the spokes. "I guess I'd better tell you something right now, before we go any further." Her voice was soft but forceful. "Nobody insults these elves and gets away with it. Not while I'm here. Nobody insults them, and nobody insults them by mistake, either," she added, seeing that Hillary was about to protest again. "Before you say anything, you've got to put yourself in the position of the elf. That way you don't make mistakes, okay?"

Hillary nodded. She leaned over and touched the Ferris wheel with the tip of her finger. She didn't want to get into another fight. The Ferris wheel was so wonderful, and besides, she could see how Sara-Kate might be right, especially if there happened to be an elf nearby listening to their conversation.

An elf nearby listening? Even as she thought this, Hillary felt an odd sensation on the back of her neck. It was as if a small hand had passed between her skin and the collar of her jacket. She glanced over her shoulder at a bush behind her.

"I know. I felt it, too," Sara-Kate said quietly, following the direction of Hillary's eyes into the bush. "I have feelings like that all the time here."

"You do? Do you think it means . . . ?"

"It's better not to talk about it," Sara-Kate whispered. "It's better to keep on doing things and not look.

"Come and see the elves' new pool!" she shouted suddenly, in a voice clearly intended for invisible ears. "It's over here! Follow me!"

Then: "Quick, come on," she whispered, and rose swiftly from her knees. Hillary rose, too, and the two girls scampered away, feeling such a pressure of elfin eyes at their backs it seemed almost that they were propelled across the yard.

That night, in bed, Hillary put her face against the window and tried to look through the dark. Now the elves were in their village. Now, if she could only see, they were walking in their front yards, sitting in their houses, talking in tiny voices among themselves. She could feel them out and about, mysterious little beings scurrying through Sara-Kate's backyard, over the broken glass, around the washing machine. Was the Ferris wheel turning? She peered into the blackness.

"Elves are almost invisible," Sara-Kate had said. "It isn't that they hide so much as that they decide not to be seen."

"But they have been seen. Some people have seen them," Hillary said. "You said so yourself."

"Right," answered Sara-Kate. "Some people. The right people. People they can trust."

"Do you think the elves could ever learn to trust us?" Hillary asked.

"That's what I'm hoping," Sara-Kate said. "But

don't count on it," she'd added immediately. "It takes a lot for an elf to get his trust working."

"But why?" Hillary had asked. "We wouldn't hurt them."

"But a lot of people have," Sara-Kate replied.

Four ✗

Sara-Kate had said "put yourself in the position of the elf." During the next week, Hillary found herself slipping into that position frequently and with remarkable ease. It did not feel odd or unnatural at all, especially with Sara-Kate hovering watchfully nearby, whispering, explaining, drawing upon an apparently endless supply of information about elves.

She knew everything that could be known about them, it seemed to Hillary, whose eyes now often followed the older girl's unusual figure at school, along halls, into classrooms. She began to wait for her near the cafeteria at lunchtime, to sit with her if Sara-Kate was willing, though she more often passed Hillary by and went to occupy a chair away by herself.

Jane Webster and Alison Mancini watched their friend's new attachment with alarm. They took Hillary aside and tried to warn her.

"What is wrong with you?" Jane hissed one day outside the lunchroom, where she had come across Hillary standing rather pathetically against the door frame. "Sara-Kate Connolly is not a good person. She's out to trick you and everybody knows it. Everybody keeps telling you to watch out, to stay away from her. But do you listen? No! You're over at her house every afternoon. You're walking home from school with her every day. And why are you standing around here waiting? She never sits with you anyway."

"Sometimes she does," Hillary replied.

Jane sighed and tried another approach.

"Have you seen what Sara-Kate eats for lunch?" she asked. "She brings white mush from home and pours sugar on top. White mush! Can you believe it?" Jane's eyes widened in horror.

"It's only Cream of Wheat cereal," Hillary answered. "Sara-Kate has a delicate stomach. She can't eat hamburgers and pizza and things like that. She cooks the Cream of Wheat herself in the morning and puts it in a thermos. That way, it's hot for lunch. She told me."

"Do you know that Sara-Kate's father is a criminal?" Alison asked Hillary later that day. "He's in prison for armed robbery and will probably be there for a long time. A friend of my mother's told her."

But Hillary only smiled. "He's not in prison, he's in Sarasota, Florida. Sara-Kate said so," she replied with such honest conviction that Alison fled to Jane in a fright.

"It's as if Sara-Kate has put a spell on her!" she whispered to her friend. "Hillary believes everything she says. Everything!"

Spell or no spell, magic or none, Hillary was getting more attached to the Connollys' backyard with each passing day. There was a lot of work to do around an elf village, she discovered. She could not just sit still and watch because even as she looked, a leaf roof would blow off and she'd have to run after it to bring it back. Or a line of pebbles would become crooked and need to be rearranged. The elves appreciated this kind of light repairwork. But they would not stand for too much meddling with their village, as Hillary soon discovered.

During a rainstorm, two of the tiny houses entirely collapsed. Hillary and Sara-Kate found them the next day. Hillary kneeled right down to begin putting the structures back together, but Sara-Kate jumped in front of her and grabbed her wrists.

"Don't touch!" she yelled. "These are elf houses and only elves can build them right. People don't know how!"

Hillary snatched her hands away angrily. "You never told me that," she said. "How am I supposed to know things you haven't even told me yet?"

"Well, it's obvious, isn't it?" Sara-Kate spat back. But then, seeing Hillary's expression, she said in a kinder voice: "It's all right. Don't worry. We can help the elves with little things. We can leave presents for them. They would like that."

"What kind of presents?" Hillard asked.

"Food!" announced Sara-Kate with a broad smile. "Elves love to eat."

Who would have thought there could be so much elf food in that brambly, neglected backyard? ("I guess that's another reason the elves came here," Hillary said to herself.)

In the brambles grew bright red berries.

"Elf apples," explained Sara-Kate, picking them off with her thin fingers.

Out of the mud appeared pure white mushrooms.

"Poisonous to humans," Sara-Kate said. "But to elves they are soft and sweet as cake."

There were also sticky green pods that contained tiny white seeds.

"Elf salt?" asked Hillary.

"Right," said Sara-Kate.

And there were blackberries and little pink flowers in the underbrush that Hillary's father would have called weed flowers. There were no weed flowers left in Hillary's backyard, and no place was muddy enough to grow mushrooms.

"You've got a perfect yard for elves," Hillary said to Sara-Kate wistfully. "Nobody in the whole neighborhood has a yard even close to this."

Sara-Kate pushed her nose up in the air. She said, "I know. I've been knowing it for a long time."

"Do elves eat regular flowers?" Hillary inquired. "We've got a whole lot of pretty ones growing in our yard."

"They hate them," Sara-Kate answered. "Regular flowers are poisonous to elves."

"I thought so," Hillary muttered. "I've been noticing that about elves."

"What?" Sara-Kate said.

"That what's poisonous to people is healthy for elves. And what people think is pretty is not at all what elves like to live near."

"You're getting to understand elves pretty well," Sara-Kate allowed. Then she found two caps off the tops of acorns that, filled with water, looked exactly like the sort of cups elves would drink out of. These they left on a leaf near the village, surrounded by all the food.

"Will it be safe?" Hillary asked, standing back to admire the banquet. "Shouldn't we cover the food with something? A dog could come along and wreck this in a minute. And it's getting so cold and windy out here," she added.

The afternoons had grown progressively chillier during the week. September was nearly over and there was a feeling of changing seasons in the air. On this particular afternoon, the wind had a nasty bite to it that now caused Hillary to turn up the collar of her thin jean jacket. Sara-Kate looked at her and shrugged.

"Don't worry," she said. "I always check things before I go to bed. And then I come look in the morning before school. It takes a lot of work to keep elves, but it's worth it."

"What will they do in winter?" Hillary asked. "They'll get pretty cold out here." Her own feet felt icy suddenly, and looking down she saw that her sneakers had gotten rather muddy.

"Elves don't get cold," Sara-Kate said.

"Everybody gets cold."

"Not elves," Sara-Kate said proudly. "They like being outside. They have thick skins. They never go inside until they have to. Houses are too hot for elves. They can't breathe right."

"Then why did they bother to build all these houses?" Hillary inquired a little sharply. She could not quite believe it about the elves' skins. Even furry animals got cold, she knew. In winter, they burrowed into caves and nests and went to sleep.

"Why don't elves just live in trees or underground like other animals?" Hillary asked Sara-Kate. "It would be so much easier for them."

Sara-Kate shook her head. "You can be pretty stupid sometimes," she scoffed. "The reason they build houses is to have a village so they can live together, of course. Elves keep together. If they lived in trees or holes, they'd be all scattered out." She squinted at Hillary. "And anyway, elves aren't animals," she added. "For one thing, they're about a hundred times smarter than any animal. They're about ten times smarter than most people and about twice as smart as a human genius."

Sara-Kate stopped suddenly and looked around toward her house. There, some signal invisible to Hillary must have caught her eye, because she began to walk rapidly in the direction of the back door.

"You've got to go home now," she told Hillary over her shoulder. "My mother wants me to come in."

When Hillary stared after her in surprise, Sara-Kate flung herself around again and bellowed, "Go on! Get going!"

She disappeared into her house with a slam of the door.

Hillary sighed. She glanced a last time at the elves' banquet to see that all was in order. She shivered. The wind had stopped coming in puffs and now blew in one long, cold stream.

All of a sudden, one of the leaf roofs came detached at one side and was blown up straight by the wind. It was a deep red color and had the curious look of a hand, fingers and thumb outstretched, waving at her. It appeared so real that Hillary wondered for a second if the elves were behind it, playing a game with her.

She smiled at this thought, and had bent down to fix the leaf when another flutter caused her to straighten up quickly and look toward Sara-Kate's house.

She saw right away what it was. A shade in one of the upstairs windows had been flicked up, and now, as she watched, a thin face rose where the shade had been and stared down at her with wide eyes. For a moment, Hillary stared back. Then she stepped away and ran for the hole in the hedge that led to her own yard.

When she reached it, she looked again but the face had vanished. The shade was already drawn back into place.

"Silly," she murmured. "It was only Sara-Kate's mother."

But the face had not looked as if it belonged to a mother, any mother. It had been too white and too thin. Too frightening.

Five ✗

The weather turned warm again. Indian summer, Hillary's mother called it, and she was happy because "I wasn't ready to close all the doors and windows yet. It's so lovely to have the fresh air! And you'll need a new winter coat," she said, measuring Hillary's ever-lengthening legs with her eyes. "Now we'll have time to shop around for the best one."

Hillary's father was happy, too. On most evenings, he left his briefcase in the hall, changed from his business suit into a pair of jeans, and went out to work in the yard. He weeded and watered and planted daffodil bulbs, whistling to himself and addressing remarks to the garden at large.

"Hot enough for you?" he'd ask if the day was a warm one. Or, after a heavy rain: "Well, we had a regular drowning party out here, I see."

"You are a nuisance," he said one evening to a group of fall roses that were beginning to shed their petals. "I just raked you out yesterday and here you've gone and dropped your underwear all over the place again."

From the hedge at the bottom of the yard, a series of muffled snorts erupted. Hillary and Sara-Kate had been crouched behind the bushes building an elf bridge across a boggy section of ground. Now they looked at each other and grinned.

"Has your father always been crazy or is this a recent problem?" Sara-Kate asked Hillary, gravely.

This brought on a second round of snorts, and a number of giggles and coughs besides.

"Everything all right down there?" Mr. Lenox called unhelpfully from the garden. It made them crack up again.

Everything was all right, of course. It couldn't have been better, in fact. Strange as it might seem, Hillary and Sara-Kate were putting together a sort of friendship. They met in Sara-Kate's backyard every afternoon to work on the elf village. Hillary's mother disapproved, but she hadn't actually forbidden the visits, so Hillary was able to slip through the hedge with the understanding that no questions would be asked.

"If you could tell me which is the poison ivy, then I can keep away from it," she'd said to Sara-Kate at the end of the first week, during which she had hardly dared venture farther than the village and the Ferris wheel. "My mother's just waiting for me to catch something down here so she can stop me from coming."

"Don't think I don't know," Sara-Kate said. She took Hillary around the yard and pointed out the worst patches, and she showed her how to recognize the poison ivy plant, with its distinctive three-leaf cluster and green sheen.

"I used to get poison ivy all the time when I was little," she said. "Then I got wise."

"Why doesn't your mother do something about it?" Hillary asked. "My father said she could get a spray to kill it if she wanted to."

"Well, she doesn't want to," Sara-Kate answered quickly, in a voice that told Hillary not to go on with the subject. It wasn't the only subject that Sara-Kate wouldn't discuss. There were many others. She was always backing out of conversations, pulling up short, telling Hillary to mind her own business. Sometimes Sara-Kate simply turned her back and walked off without explanation, as she'd done on the day when Hillary had seen the face in the window. Being friends with Sara-Kate was a complicated business. But sometimes . . .

Behind the hedge, Hillary looked over at Sara-Kate, who was still laughing about the roses' underwear, and thought what a nice person she was when she let herself relax. She was really no different from anyone else, Hillary decided. She even managed to look rather pretty at times, after one got to know her and could ignore her boots and the strange clothes she wore.

The project underway at the elf village that afternoon was the construction of a network of roads or paths leading to different parts of the yard. The elves were a quick, energetic people who needed to be able to move around easily, Sara-Kate had explained. But they were not, by nature, roadbuilders, preferring to follow the trails made by other animals. There were no animals living in Sara-Kate's backyard, just a few squirrels whose road-ways ran overhead, along the branches of two ragged trees.

"So we must take over the job of making roads," Sara-Kate informed Hillary. "And what I was think-ing was, we could make a really good system. First we could design a plan for where the roads should go, and then we could carry it out."

"If you want me to make a map, I'm good at that," Hillary replied. "I studied maps in school last year. I know about scales and ledgers and things."

"Good," Sara-Kate said.

So, as official map-maker, Hillary had walked the boundaries of Sara-Kate's yard with a pad and pen-cil. She had marked the position of the overturned washing machine, of large bushes, trees, tree stumps, and of such smaller landmarks as derelict tires, rusty pipes, oil cans, and ash heaps. She noted the placement of the back porch and discovered the swampy area near the hedge, which was too soft to support a road and might be dangerous to a small being like an elf.

While she walked, watching her step for fear of broken glass or poison ivy, Hillary kept half an eye on the blank, shade-drawn windows of Sara-Kate's house, especially the upstairs windows. For there, at times, some tiny movement, an almost impercep-tible flutter, seemed to catch her attention, and she would whirl around to look with a leaping heart.

But whether it was her imagination or a reflection trick of the window glass, she could never positively identify what had moved, or where. And she did not dare ask Sara-Kate about such things. She would only have laughed or become angry. She might even have ordered Hillary out of the yard for good, a possibility that worried Hillary far more than the feeling that she was being secretly observed.

Short of being ordered away, Hillary wouldn't have stopped coming to the yard for anything. The place fascinated her, and she liked the idea that she was beginning to know its parts: the stumps, the rocks, the junk heaps, and the hidden places where the tiny weed flowers bloomed. She liked knowing how to get around and between obstacles—how to steer clear of thorn bushes, for instance, by walking the trunk of a fallen tree. She had a feeling of belonging to the yard, even of owning it a little.

The Lenoxes' tidy yard belonged to her father and mother, Hillary saw. It was under their order and grew according to their laws. But Sara-Kate's yard was wild and free, and that was how Hillary felt there, tramping among the bushes, poking into shadowy dens. Anything might happen in Sara-Kate's backyard. For that matter, anything *was* happening.

The elves might keep themselves hidden. They might even be invisible to the human eye, as Sara-Kate believed. But everywhere, everywhere! there was evidence of their small, exotic lives.

A cache of acorn cups would turn up in the hollow of a tree root, leading Hillary to imagine an industrious band of little workers moving and storing goods throughout the garden.

Several odd, circular dirt clearings appeared in the weedy underbrush. The earth of these places was packed firm and level, and, though no footprints or marks showed there, it seemed obvious that these were meeting areas of some sort.

But why? What did the elves discuss? What language did they speak? Did they talk in words, or did communication take place through some form of silent sign language? After all, there was never a mutter or a cough in the yard, not during the day and not at night either, according to Sara-Kate. There was only the sound of the wind moving through bushes and tree boughs.

"If I were an elf and wanted to speak so that no one would hear me, I would make up a language that sounded like ordinary natural sounds," Sara-Kate had said.

"What sounds?" Hillary asked.

"Be quiet and listen for a minute." They had stood still until the tiny noises within the boundaries of the yard began to distinguish themselves from the louder noises of the town: from traffic passing in the street, the shriek of brakes, the cries of children and yapping of dogs.

Underneath these town noises, Hillary heard tiny chirps and squeaks. She heard a faint vibration or buzz coming through the air. She heard pecking and tapping noises, little creaks and scratches, groans and gushes, clickings and drippings. Finally, she heard the clear notes of a bird, very close by.

"Is that an elf talking?" she whispered in amazement.

Sara-Kate shrugged. "It could be. Who can tell?"

Hillary had nodded. It might very well be. But of course, with elves it was impossible to be sure of anything. One might suppose that certain things were happening, that the elves acted in a certain way, but who could really tell? Facts can be understood differently, they can add up to different answers depending on how they are viewed.

This uncertainty about the elves had come home to Hillary after a particularly interesting conversation with Sara-Kate one day, a conversation about the strange little pool the elves had made for themselves out of an old tin pan sunk in the ground near the Ferris wheel.

At night in the dark, or perhaps in faint moonlight, the elves bathed in the pool. Hillary knew they bathed because she saw fresh seeds and half-eaten berries near the water's edge. She saw small, square pieces of wood floating in the water, along with tiny, yellow leaves that seemed to have no source within the yard.

What purpose did the wooden pieces serve? Hillary wondered. And what about the leaves?

After some thought, she had come up with an answer. The wooden squares were rafts upon which the elves sat or lay, and the leaves were washcloths, because the elves must have some means of washing, mustn't they? It seemed most likely.

But Sara-Kate had laughed when she heard Hillary's ideas.

"Why do you think that these elves are anything like you?" she asked. "You play with rafts in pools and you use washcloths, so you think elves must, too. But maybe elves aren't like you at all. Maybe they're so different that nothing they do is anything like what you do. Maybe they've never even seen a washcloth and these leaves are for something else, for collecting starlight, say."

"Collecting starlight! Why?"

"Maybe for energy to run things, the way we use the sun for solar energy."

"To run what?"

"Well, there's the Ferris wheel. Suppose the wood pieces aren't water rafts but power rafts. Maybe the swimming pool isn't for swimming at all. It could be a power center that collects energy and stores it for future use. I'm not saying this is true," Sara-Kate added hastily. "I'm just trying to show you what's possible."

Hillary was astounded. Starlight collectors! She would never have imagined such a thing and she looked with respect at Sara-Kate. Not that she was convinced about the power rafts, but she saw that Sara-Kate was right in principle. She must not take anything for granted when it came to an unknown like elves. She must just watch and wait and hope that they would reveal themselves more clearly.

In the meantime, the road and bridge project went forward in the afternoons until most parts of the yard had been linked with the elf village. But Indian summer soon passed and the days grew shorter and colder, making it less pleasant to work outside.

Less pleasant especially for Sara-Kate, Hillary thought. She stubbornly refused to put on any kind of coat. While Hillary arrived wearing sweaters and jackets and finally a new quilted parka, Sara-Kate went on working in her same blue sweatshirt, which by this time was looking rather ragged around the cuffs.

"Aren't you cold?" Hillary asked her. On some afternoons, there was a thin layer of ice on the elves' pool.

"No," Sara-Kate answered.

"Are you trying to act like an elf and have thick skin?" Hillary said, teasing a little.

Sara-Kate had turned on her in one of her unpredictable bursts of fury.

"For your information, I'm not trying to act like anything. I happen to be like an elf, that's all. I don't get cold. If you think that's weird, why don't you go away and tell your stupid friends about it."

But, of course, Hillary chose not to go away.

Six

In all the time that Hillary had been going to Sara-Kate's backyard to work on the elf village, Sara-Kate had never once invited her inside her house.

Never once had she offered Hillary a soda or a snack. She had never asked her in to see her room, or to watch television. When it rained, Hillary went home. When she got hungry, Hillary went back to her own kitchen.

"Do you want something?" she'd ask Sara-Kate. "We have cupcakes." Or she'd offer an apple, popcorn, lemonade, for Mrs. Lenox believed in a well-stocked larder and kept many delicious snacks on her shelves.

But Sara-Kate never wanted anything. Elf banquets were one thing. For herself, she did not seem interested in food. She didn't like to watch Hillary eating either, or so it seemed, for she would turn away and go off to another part of the yard while Hillary nibbled around the edges of a raspberry fruit pie or a chocolate-chip cookie she had brought from home. It was as if Sara-Kate found the sight of this sort of food disgusting.

On the other hand, Hillary occasionally caught

her tossing a handful of yard berries into her mouth when she thought no one was looking. And she often munched on mint leaves from a patch of mint grown wild near the back porch.

"Elves chew mint like gum," she told Hillary once.

Hillary watched Sara-Kate chewing and guessed that her odd tastes were another instance of her being "like an elf."

"If you ask me, Sara-Kate *is* an elf," Jane said in a nasty voice to Hillary at school. "She's a mean, dirty little elf who's put a spell on you and is going to get you in trouble, wait and see."

Jane and Alison were angry at Hillary and she was angry at them.

"You think you're so great because a big fifth grader is your friend," Alison hissed. "But nobody in the whole school likes Sara-Kate. Nobody else wants to hang around her horrible old house. There's not even any furniture in there, did you know? Somebody sneaked up and looked through the window one day. There aren't any chairs or anything."

"Sara-Kate is your friend because she can't get anybody else," Jane added. "She got you by telling you a lot of lies about elves. Why are you so stupid, Hillary?"

"Shut up," Hillary replied. "Sara-Kate isn't lying. And she has beautiful furniture. Whoever said she didn't is the one who's lying. I've been in her house hundreds of times so I should know."

Not only had Hillary never seen the inside of Sara-Kate's house, she had not seen Sara-Kate's mother since the day she'd stared out the second floor window for that brief moment. Mrs. Connolly never came out of the house. She never came to the door to call Hillary inside. She never made a sound.

And yet, she was there. Hillary knew it. Besides the way the shades moved at times—as if someone were crouched behind them watching the activity in the yard—there were the errands that Sara-Kate was constantly being sent to do.

Hillary had even begun to accompany her: to the drugstore to pick up a prescription; to the post office; to the little grocery store two blocks away for a bunch of carrots, a half gallon of milk, a box of Saltines. Hillary went secretly, of course. Her parents would never have allowed her to walk around the town, which was more like a small city in the downtown sections. They would have worried about traffic on the busy streets, about the beckoning finger of a stranger. They would have worried that Hillary would become lost, or get bitten by one of the homeless dogs that roamed the trashy alleys, or fall into a hole and lie there unconscious and ignored.

Apparently Sara-Kate's mother worried about none of these possibilities. Hillary wondered if she knew where Sara-Kate was half the time. And naturally Sara-Kata didn't worry. Perhaps she'd never been told about the terrible things that can happen to a child alone on the streets. She went to the laundromat to wash clothes, to the hardware store to "make a payment," to the bank to cash a check.

Hillary watched Sara-Kate's small figure transact these grown-up pieces of business with increasing amazement. After all, Sara-Kate was no bigger than Hillary, and though she was two years older, she did not look old enough to be so effective in the adult world. But effective she was, although Hillary once heard her questioned by a woman in the business office of the telephone company, where she had gone to restart telephone service that had been shut off at her house.

"Where is your mother?" the woman inquired sharply. "She should be handling this."

"She's sick, so she had to send me," Sara-Kate replied quickly. The telephone official regarded her doubtfully, but she accepted the pile of money that Sara-Kate placed on her desk.

"How do you know what to do?" Hillary asked Sara-Kate later. "Do you do everything for your mother?"

"Not everything. Just what she tells me."

So Sara-Kate's mother was sick. That scrap of information was among the few that Hillary managed to glean during her month of visiting the Connollys' backyard. Sara-Kate almost never spoke about herself. She never told stories about her family. If Hillary forgot and questioned her too closely on some personal matter, Sara-Kate snapped at her. Or she was silent, as if she had not heard.

· 43

"What sickness does your mother have?"
Silence.
"Are you the only child in your family, like me?"
Silence.
"Why was your telephone shut off?"
Silence.

Only about the elf village and the elves themselves did Sara-Kate became talkative and open. In fact, as time went on, the mysterious world of the elves became clearer and clearer in Hillary's mind from Sara-Kate's telling about it, and Hillary could almost see the pale, quick-as-a-wink faces peer out from the underbrush.

Perhaps she had seen one, or rather part of one. As Sara-Kate explained, the elfin trick of invisibility depended to a great extent on their never appearing whole before humans. Sara-Kate herself saw bits and pieces of elves everywhere in the yard: a flash of arm, a pointed foot, an eye, wheaten hair blowing in the wind like yellow grass.

"It isn't where you look for elves so much as how you look," she advised one day when Hillary had despaired of ever seeing the little people. "You've got to train yourself to notice details. You can't just stomp around the place expecting to be shown things. Go slowly and quietly, and look deep."

So Hillary went slowly and quietly. She began to look deep into the bushes of Sara-Kate's yard, deep into piles of leaves, into hedges. The yard seemed more open now because the trees and bushes had shed their leaves. She saw holes, hollows, and stumps that hadn't been visible under all the foliage.

"I think I just saw an elbow!" she would call to Sara-Kate, who would turn toward her skeptically.

"Are you sure?" she'd ask. "Are you really sure?"

"Yes!" Hillary would cry, but she wasn't. She was never sure what she had seen. It was maddening.

Hillary found herself bringing her new noticing eyes back home with her to her own yard. She noticed, for instance, how the ivy climbing her father's birdbath turned brittle, then brown, and began to lose its grip on the fluted stem.

She saw an abandoned nest in the bare branches of the apple tree. She noticed how evening came earlier and earlier, until it was completely dark when her father returned home from his office and there was no time for him to work in his garden. But then again, she saw that frost had killed the flowers and the grass had stopped growing so there was no reason for him to go out there anyway.

At the dinner table, Mr. Lenox looked tired and talked about people who weren't doing their jobs at work. When Hillary's fork dropped on her plate with a crash by mistake, he jumped and scowled at her. Looking deep, Hillary thought she knew why.

"He misses his garden," she whispered to herself.

"You're so quiet these days I hardly know when you're in the house or out," Hillary's mother said to her. "Would you like to invite Jane or Alison over for the night this weekend? Or how about both!" Mrs. Lenox offered, a little wildly, because Hillary had been worrying her lately.

"You're spending far too much time in the Connollys' yard," she might have added, but didn't since the subject was an embarrassing one. Mrs. Lenox disliked the Connollys' shabbiness. She was nervous about the disorder lurking just beyond the hedge. It nibbled at the edges of her own well-kept yard. But how could she speak to Hillary about the unsuitableness of such a house, such a family? She couldn't. Hillary looked deep and heard her anyway.

"I can't come here every day anymore," she told Sara-Kate. "My mother is noticing it too much."

Sara-Kate shrugged. "Do what you want," she replied, as if she didn't care. Then her small eyes scurried to Hillary's face to see what could be read there.

"I want to come," Hillary said, meeting her gaze. "It isn't me that wants to stay away. It's my mother."

"Sure, I know," Sara-Kate answered. "You don't have to say it. I already know."

Hillary often wondered about Sara-Kate's life inside her gloomy house. In early November she finally got a chance to see. Even then, it wasn't by invitation but because no one would come to answer the door. She'd knocked and knocked. She'd stepped back near the elf village and tried calling up to the second floor.

"Sara-Kate!" she bellowed. "It's me! What's wrong?"

Not one sound came from anywhere inside and an odd little fright had crept into Hillary. The day was icy and dark. She jumped up and down to keep her feet from freezing. The yard lay around her, hunched under the cold. Bushes whose languid shapes she had come to know well in warmer weather now posed in awkward positions, their scrawny limbs angled and bent.

"Sara-Kate, where are you!"

Sara-Kate had not come to school for three days. Hillary couldn't remember her ever missing before. Odder still, she had not been outside working on the elf village when Hillary had come through the hedge to visit on Monday afternoon. That day, Hillary had gone home quietly. And she had gone home again on Tuesday when Sara-Kate had not appeared in the yard, but with uneasy feelings.

"Are the Connollys away?" she asked her mother, a ridiculous question since Mrs. Lenox had no more knowledge of the Connollys' comings and goings than of a family in Outer Mongolia.

"I thought we might go to the shoe store this afternoon to find something pretty for you to wear at Thanksgiving," her mother said, presenting such a happy prospect that Hillary forgot to worry about Sara-Kate for the rest of the day.

But on Wednesday there was again no sign of her and so, in the afternoon, Hillary approached the Connollys' back door and bravely knocked. Her fist made such a tiny, hollow noise—it was as if the house were completely empty—that she began to pound with the flat of her hand. There was no door-bell and no knocker.

"Sara-Kate!" Clouds of breath exploded from her

mouth. Behind her the yard was silent, listening. Or perhaps it didn't listen. Hillary looked over her shoulder. Perhaps it was as empty as the house. Not a twig moved. Not a bird chirped. In the elf village, many cottages were falling apart. The Ferris wheel stood grandly over the ground, but brush and debris had blown into its wires and the Popsicle-stick seats were tossed and tangled.

Hillary put her mittened hand on the doorknob and turned. The door came open.

"Sara-Kate?" she asked softly of the darkness within. Then, since there was no answer here either, she stepped forward across the threshold.

Seven ✓

If, by some charm, Hillary had been shrunk to a height of three inches and escorted through the door of one of Sara-Kate's elf houses, it would have seemed no stranger than the place she entered now. Certainly, whatever peculiarities an elf house might have had—stars adrift near the ceiling, hypnotized moths on the walls?—it would have been more welcoming. This room was cold as ice, and dim. Hillary could distinguish little at first, just a heap of mysteriously shaped objects rising from the floor in front of her.

Gradually, as her eyes adjusted, she made out a table and then two bulky chairs from the heap. A cardboard box, a floor lamp, a stool, and a low bookcase came into view. They were set in a sort of circle in the middle of the room and, at their center, most incongruous of all, was a large white stove. But what a strange-looking stove. Hillary took a step nearer. The oven had no door, only a cavernous mouth where the door should have been. And the burners on top were gone, leaving behind four empty craters.

An electric fan was perched on a bureau positioned next to the stove. The bureau's drawers had been removed, however, to serve other functions. Hillary caught sight of one in the corner being used

· 49

as a container for tools. Another, turned upside-down over a stool, had become a table top. Meanwhile, the bureau's drawer slots had become storage holes for cooking pans, jars, utensils, newspapers, and other items unidentifiable in the poor light.

In fact, everything in the room seemed to have been dismantled, rearranged, and transformed into something else, Hillary noticed during the full minute she stood gazing about just inside the back door. She saw that the room had been an ordinary kitchen once. There was a refrigerator against the far wall, and a sink and faucet were visible beneath a window whose torn shade allowed outside light to enter. For the rest, everything not actually attached to the wall or the floor (the radiator was still in place for instance) had been uprooted and dragged to the room's center, where it was installed around the stove to make another room. A room within a room.

But now, even this odd inner room seemed to have fallen into disuse. Hillary walked around it cautiously, examining its different sides. The two shabby armchairs, worn to cotton stuffing in the seats, had been pushed so close to the stove's open mouth that the people sitting in them must have baked their legs if the oven had been turned on. Hillary drew her mittened hand along a chair back. A fine dust rose.

Sara-Kate and her mother had gone away, this much was clear. The house was shut down. The heat was turned off. They had gone to visit friends or perhaps they were in Sarasota, Florida, with Sara-

Kate's father. They had left quickly, without telling anyone, and they had forgotten to lock the back door. Not that there was anything here to steal. Never had Hillary seen a place so stripped of the basic comforts.

She finished circling the inner room and arrived back near the door. But instead of opening it and going home, she walked across the floor to a doorway on the other side that led to another room. She could understand now why Sara-Kate had never wanted to invite her in.

The second room was completely empty and made her remember Alison's report on the state of the house. The walls were bare, the windows had no curtains, and when Hillary walked in, the sounds her feet made on the hardwood floor were as loud as hammer blows. The smallest sniff or rustle was magnified by the emptiness into an alarming hiss. She examined the room's yellowed window shades, all drawn but one that had fallen askew. She noticed the dust lying black on the sills, the cobwebs trailing from the ceiling. This was not a room recently cleared of its contents. This room had lain empty for months, maybe years, accumulating mold and rot and insect bodies, of which there were hundreds on the floor, Hillary saw. She stepped to one side with distaste. Had this been a dining room once? An ancient film of flowered wallpaper coated the walls.

She was near another doorway now, and through it she saw the shadowy lines of a staircase leading to the second floor. She did not want to go there. The cold in Sara-Kate's house was intense. Hillary pushed her mittened hands into her parka pockets and hunched her shoulders. Her nose and cheeks were icy. She turned back to the kitchen and had already taken several steps in the direction of the back door when she stopped. A faint noise reached her ears. It was just barely audible through her wooly hat. She took her hands from her pockets and pulled the hat off.

The sound was coming from somewhere above her, a series of little thumps as if something were being knocked or rolled upon the floor. The noises stopped as she listened, then started again a few seconds later. Hillary's heart jumped.

Perhaps she had been frightened all along and not noticed. The house had seemed more odd than threatening, more closed up and left behind than eerie. But maybe, all the time, protective antennae in Hillary had been picking up warning signals: a wisp of a smell, a current of air, a sigh, an echo. For suddenly she knew she was not alone in Sara-Kate's house. Someone was here with her.

Above, the sounds stopped again. Hillary held her breath and stood absolutely still. She calculated the direction of the noises, and was looking up, toward the back rear corner of the old kitchen, when they began again—a rolling, a knocking—just where she was staring. The sounds were coming through the ceiling from the second floor.

Hillary knew she should run. She thought of racing for the back door, flinging it open, crossing Sara-Kate's yard in three strides and without looking back crashing through the hedge into her own safe garden. Sara-Kate's house was too cold and dark for any usual sort of being to be living in it. But in that case, Hillary reasoned in a rush of thoughts, the source of the noises must be some thing or things unusual. It must be some thing or things with fur coats or hot blood for staying warm. Or perhaps possessing thick skins?

Hillary didn't move. She stared at the ceiling. She remembered how empty the yard had seemed these last three days. She thought of the elf village, whose houses were beginning to collapse, whose leaf roofs were blown away. Their fragile construction had never been intended for winter living. She recalled Sara-Kate's words: "Elves never go inside until they have to. . . ." *Until they have to.* And with Sara-Kate and her mother away, the house must have seemed the most logical place to go.

Over her head, the little roly-knocking noises had stopped again. In the silence, Hillary found herself turning quietly and tiptoeing through the door into the vacant dining room, across its dusty floor, and beyond another door. She came to the foot of the dark staircase in a hall so bitterly cold that it seemed to her the ice heart of the whole frozen house.

Hillary crept upward, stair by stair. She moved slowly and made little noise. The stair boards are too cold to squeak, she thought. She took shallow breaths to quiet the sound of her breathing and was lightheaded when she reached the top. Here, she paused, holding onto the banister.

A dark corridor swept past her. Away to the left, she heard the noises begin again, but for a little while she stayed where she was, drawing in gulps of icy black air. She was not frightened now, but filled with anticipation. Her fear was that the elves would hear her coming with their quick, pointed ears. She was sure they would perform some vanishing trick if they suspected her presence. Or they would run or fly away. Her plan was to burst suddenly into the room, to catch them unaware for a moment. And in that moment, Hillary would see an elf whole at last, which even Sara-Kate had never done.

Hillary leaned on the banister and tried to imagine what the elves would look like. She prepared herself for their small bodies, for their elf-made clothes—little hats and coats, little shoes with curly tips. For some reason, she had imagined them dressed in a bright spring green, but now she realized this might be another case of coming to the wrong conclusions. More likely, elves change color with the seasons, like chameleons, Hillary thought. She smiled. She was ready for anything. Sara-Kate's elves might have pink hair and purple eyes for all she cared. She was ready.

At last Hillary's breath steadied and she began to feel her way down the corridor. She moved with agonizing slowness, keeping one hand on the wall for balance. The noises had continued on and off during the time she had rested, but there was no need to listen to discover which room they came from. On the right-hand side, about halfway down the hall, light streamed beneath a closed door. It was not a pale, mysterious light, but a fiery yellow one. It poured through the keyhole as well, and through the cracks at the door's edges. To Hillary, approaching down the dark hallway, there seemed a great pressure of light upon this door, so that it bulged with the effort of holding the brightness in.

Or was magic what was being contained? Hillary came forward and stood before the throbbing door as if drawn by a magnet. She stared at the plain brown wood. Her mittened hand rose to encircle the doorknob and turn it slowly. The roly-knocking noises continued while the door came silently open and the room was revealed in a rush of heat and light.

Hillary did not believe what she saw. She looked again and again and could not understand. Then she understood. The elves had played a trick on her after all. They had sensed her coming at the final moment and vanished through the walls. They had substituted another scene to confuse her.

Before Hillary's dazzled eyes sat Sara-Kate Connolly in a black rocking chair holding a long-legged figure in her arms. The figure's feet were dragging on the floor as Sara-Kate rocked back and forth. The figure's face was sad and white. Its hands clung to one of Sara-Kate's hands. Oh those elves! They were so ingenious. They had changed their own roly-knocking noises (the sounds of tiny feet, of mysterious wheels) into the noise a rocking chair makes against a bare wood floor. They had changed themselves into Sara-Kate and—who was it?—her mother? Hillary's hands flew up to cover her mouth. It was all so ridiculous!

At the same time, the scene in the room came to life. Sara-Kate's bullet eyes zipped across the floor. They shot into Hillary with a force that made her gasp. This was no trick. Sara-Kate had no sooner seen Hillary than she began to struggle to her feet. She lifted the thin figure from her lap and laid it in the chair. She whirled and rushed across the room.

"Out!" Sara-Kate screamed. "Why are you here? Get out!"

She leapt at Hillary like a wild animal, as if she meant to tear her to pieces.

"Sara-Kate! It's me!" Hillary tried to say, but her voice was strangled by surprise.

"Get away! Go back home!" Sara-Kate screamed. She grabbed Hillary's coat with both hands and pushed her out the door. Then she dragged her along the hall and tried to shove her down the stairs.

"Stop it!" Hillary cried. "It's me. It's me."

Sara-Kate did stop. She stopped long enough to pull Hillary's face up close to hers and to hiss like a furious snake.

"You get out and don't come back," Sara-Kate hissed in this new, horrible voice. "Forget you ever came here. Erase it from your mind. It didn't happen. You were never in this house."

Hillary stared at her in horror. She turned and began to run down the stairs.

"If you come back, you can bet you'll never go home again," Sara-Kate yelled behind her. "And if you tell anybody anything, even one little thing, that'll be the end. The end of you, I mean. The awful end. The final end. If you dare say one word to anyone on this earth, I'll . . ."

Hillary didn't wait to hear the details of what Sara-Kate was going to do to her. She was on her way out the back door at last. And she was crossing the Connollys' yard in three strides, and she was crashing through the hedge, back into her own safe garden.

Eight ✗

There were times during the next week when Hillary thought she must have dreamed her visit to Sara-Kate's house. Certainly it was dream-like enough—a shadowy staircase, a secret room, a sense of unreality, of having been in a fantasy. For dreams, like fantasies, take place only in your head. Whatever happens in them, they stay in your head and leave few signs of themselves in real life.

So it was with this frightening visit. Though Hillary seemed to have been inside Sara-Kate's house, and though certain shocking events appeared to have happened, now her life went on in the most ordinary way, made up of the most ordinary things. Day after day, she did her homework, shopped at the supermarket with her mother, brushed her teeth, and combed her hair. Night after night, she watched television, was kissed good night by her parents, and fell asleep in her bed. Nothing was changed, and furthermore nothing was changed at Sara-Kate's house. It continued to look as it had always looked—gray, gloomy, in need of repair. At night, the windows were as dark as ever.

At school, people said that Sara-Kate had gone away with her mother on a trip. With relief, Hillary believed it must be true. There was no sign of her anywhere. No one came out of her house and no one went in. No one came to look after the elf village, or to fix the Ferris wheel, which had blown off the cinder blocks during a rain storm and lay on its side in the dirt. (Hillary had peeked through the hedge and seen it.)

No one talked about Sara-Kate, either. Now that she was not on hand to scandalize people with her gas-station boots, or to yell, or to sit by herself eating mush at lunchtime, there was no reason to discuss her. Sara-Kate Connolly was gone. Hillary had had a dream. The school office had received a note from Mrs. Connolly withdrawing her daughter from school, someone said. There was no need to look into the matter more deeply.

But when Hillary really thought about it, she knew she hadn't dreamed the empty house. She knew she'd been awake when she climbed the dark stairs. She knew the second-floor room had been real.

Hillary didn't want to think about these things. Hadn't she been told to forget?

"You were never in this house!" Sara-Kate had screamed. Now Hillary tried to make it so. She closed certain doors in her mind. She turned certain locks. She shut off the lights and walked away. But the memory of Sara-Kate holding her mother in the rocking chair in the upstairs bedroom would not be locked up. It followed her around like a determined dog.

"Go away! Go away!" Hillary whispered to this dog of a memory.

"What?" Jane Webster would ask.

"Did you say something?" Alison Mancini would demand.

She was back with her friends, and happy to be back. They were wearing their star jackets in school again, and when they walked down the hall, it was always three abreast and shoulders touching. They were the Three Musketeers, they said. Alison's mother had persuaded her to cut her hair off short as a boy's around the ears, and now Alison was trying to persuade the other Musketeers to have it done.

"You just walk in and ask for an Eton cut," she said. "They know how to do them there."

"Where?" Jane inquired.

"At the place my mother goes. They do everything, nails, eyebrows, skin. My mother had a facial the last time she went. They put these layers of cream on your face and massage it around and then wrap everything up in a hot towel. It makes your skin come out really soft and nice, like a brand new skin. The old, ugly skin just peels right off."

Alison glanced at Hillary. "You're whispering to yourself again," she informed her coldly, "and it's driving me crazy."

"What is it?" Jane asked with a concerned look. "You can tell us. We can tell each other everything. We're supposed to tell each other, in fact. That's part of being a Musketeer. Listen, Alison, that gives me an idea. How about writing down some rules for ourselves, and then we can sign them and swear to obey, and then . . ."

"Go away. Go away," Hillary told the memory of Sara-Kate under her breath.

Whenever she thought of Sara-Kate in the second-floor room, Hillary thought immediately of the elves. She had expected the elves to be there. More than that, she had known they were there. She had felt their presence in the house as strongly as she felt the presence of her own mother when she was out of sight in another part of the Lenoxes' house. Hillary might not be able to see her mother but she could tell when she was nearby, working at some job, humming, making little tapping and rustling noises that were distinctly hers.

"Do you think I could have gone up those stairs without knowing what was up there?" she would have protested to Jane and Alison if the subject had been one she could talk about.

"Do you think I could have sneaked down that dark hall? The elves were there. They were in that room. They were there and then . . ."

Here Hillary came to an impasse. The elves had vanished and Sara-Kate and her mother had appeared. How could such a thing happen?

Evidence can have several different meanings, she remembered Sara-Kate teaching her. It can add up to different answers depending on how it is looked at. And that seemed the only way the problem could be resolved. For when Hillary added up the evidence on one side, it came to one unmistakable answer: elves! But when she looked at the facts from another point of view, there was no possible explanation but that Sara-Kate and her mother had been in that room all the time. Could both views somehow be true at once?

Whatever the case, neither Sara-Kate nor the elves had returned to repair the village. Hillary crept back to look again, under cover of evening. The little houses were more broken than before. The big house and the yard were silent, abandoned. She looked up to the window on the second floor and there, for a terrifying moment, she thought she saw something. A shape darker than the dim space of the window materialized before her eyes. Then it dissolved, became a trick of the mind. Sara-Kate was gone. The elves were gone. There was nothing, nothing in that old empty house.

"Go away. Go away," Hillary whispered. She flattened her hands against her ears and held them there.

"What?" her mother said.

"Were you talking to me?" her father asked.

"Hillary! What is wrong with you!" shrieked Jane and Alison. "If you have something to tell us, then tell us!"

Another week went by. A light snow fell. Ice formed on the town pond. In the cellar of the Lenoxes' house, Mr. Lenox started a building project.

"I'm making a trellis," he said to Hillary one night, after she had come down the gritty cellar stairs to see what all the pounding was about. "It's for the garden. I'm going to plant a trumpet vine near the house next spring and it will need something to climb on. It will need something to throw its long green arms around and pull itself up on inch by inch toward the sun until it has filled every space with leaves and produced the most brilliant orange trumpet flowers you've ever seen! Oh, yes, trumpet flowers!" Mr. Lenox crowed, while Hillary looked at him in alarm.

"I've been dreaming about trumpet vines at night," he added sheepishly. "Last night I dreamed I *was* one." He glanced at Hillary. "Do you miss your elf garden as much as I miss my garden?" he asked.

Hillary shrugged. "It wasn't really a garden," she said. "The only flowers were weed flowers, and there was a lot of junk lying around, but . . ."

Her father nodded. "I guess everybody has a private idea of what makes a good garden," he said. "Now, for me, the Connollys' backyard doesn't amount to much, and your mother thinks Sara-Kate isn't the best of all possible friends you could have . . ."

"But she is!" Hillary exclaimed with a sudden burst of warmth. "She is the best possible. I know it's hard to see, but Sara-Kate is a wonderful person. She's taught me all kinds of things. And she's talented, though she doesn't like to show it. Do you know she can walk on her hands? She walked up and down her driveway one time, and even up the steps of her porch. I couldn't believe it. But she never would do it again. She gets mad a lot if you say the wrong thing and then . . ."

Hillary stopped and glanced suspiciously at her father. It was the first time she'd told anyone about her feelings for Sara-Kate and now, having told this much, she felt a terrible temptation to continue. A flock of words was rising inside her. A hundred small details about Sara-Kate's habits and their work together, about the long, cool afternoons at the elf village sprang into her mind and she wanted to tell them.

But on the heels of the hundred details came the hundred questions. They were the questions that Sara-Kate had refused to answer and the ones that Hillary had learned not to ask. They were the questions she must never ask her parents or her friends, because to ask would be to tell and to tell about Sara-Kate was unthinkable.

Hillary pressed her lips together and stopped talking. She looked down at her father, who was on his knees working over the trellis. She saw Sara-Kate come charging at her out of the upstairs room, yelling, grabbing her, shoving her—almost down the stairs!—and her eyes filled with tears.

"You didn't need to do that," Hillary wanted to tell her. "I wouldn't have told. You could have said anything and I'd have understood. You didn't need to go away. You could have trusted me."

Mr. Lenox cleared his throat and half-turned toward his daughter.

"I saw Sara-Kate the other night, out late, coming home from somewhere," he said. "Running home, I should say. I almost drove into her crossing the Valley Road intersection."

Hillary stared at her father. "You saw Sara-Kate?"

"Probably out on another errand for her mother. It's a shame how she orders that child around."

"It couldn't have been Sara-Kate you saw," Hillary said. "She's not here. She's on a trip with her mother. Or maybe she's living somewhere else by now. They went away more than two weeks ago."

"It was Sara-Kate all right. She ran directly in front of my headlights. I jammed on the brakes, but she got out of the way in time."

Hillary watched her father, who was crouched over, pounding a nail.

"When was this?"

"A couple of nights ago." He took another nail from his pocket and hammered it in. The structure on the floor quivered with each blow.

"Wait a minute, I know exactly when it was," Mr. Lenox said, sitting up. "It was three days ago, last Monday about eleven o'clock at night. I was coming home from that town council meeting. I guess she came back without telling you," he said to Hillary.

"But she couldn't have. She's not there."

"How do you know?" Mr. Lenox asked.

Hillary felt a stab of fright in her chest. Then a stab of longing.

"She's not at school," she told her father. "If she'd come back, she'd be at school, right?"

Mr. Lenox took out another nail, lined it up, and hammered it in.

"Well, all I know is what I saw," he said. He rose to his feet with a grunt, picked up the half-made trellis, and handed it to Hillary. "Hold this thing up straight so I can measure it," he said, "and I'll tell you how Sara-Kate went home that night. She turned down Congdon Street, cut across the Briggs's yard to Hoover Street, cut through the Smythes' yard on the corner of Hoover and Willow, and ran into her own yard and around back of the house. I saw her go. I had to go the same way in the car to get home and I kept seeing her ahead, running in the dark. It was impressive, I must say. I'd never seen a person that small run so fast."

Nine ✘

Hillary slipped out the back door of her house like a fugitive, her quilted jacket rolled up and clutched to her chest. Behind her, she heard her father start to hammer again in the cellar. She closed the door quickly, went down the porch steps, and walked to a place away from the house where the porch light did not shine on her. Here she stopped and put on the jacket, zipping it tight around her neck. She groped for her mittens in the pockets.

The night air was frigid. The temperature was going down to ten degrees, and more snow was on the way. Her parents had talked about it during dinner. The storm might come as early as tomorrow morning.

"Welcome to winter," her mother had said cheerfully. "Maybe they'll have to cancel school," she'd added, smiling at Hillary.

Her wooly hat was in her pocket but the mittens were missing. Hillary wondered if they had dropped on the closet floor when she'd gone to snatch her coat, ready to leap into the closet herself if her mother appeared. Mrs. Lenox was upstairs reading, but it was too risky to go back now. The clock in the kitchen had showed just past 9:00 p.m., which was Hillary's bedtime, though her parents sometimes forgot and allowed her to stay up later. One thing they would never allow, however, was an unexplained, late-night walk in the cold by herself.

Hillary's unprotected hands were already stinging. She pulled the sleeves of her jacket down over them and gathered the sleeve ends with her fingers to close the openings. Then she walked across the driveway and went downhill into the dark. As she moved, her eyes sought the black bulk of Sara-Kate's house, and when she'd found that, she leveled her gaze at the second floor, to the windows just under the line of the roof. And when those were picked out (for her eyes took several minutes to accustom themselves to the darkness), she looked straight at the one window, the window on the right overlooking the yard, and beamed all her powers of detection there. If Sara-Kate was inside, Hillary was going to find out this very night, this very hour, because no one—not even elves—can stay inside a house at night in total darkness. And if there is a light, even the faintest candlelight, even the smallest flashlight, it will inevitably show up to those looking in from outside.

Hillary knew how ingenious light can be at escaping, because of her own attempts to read under her covers or inside her closet after she'd been put to bed.

"But how did you know!" she would wail when her mother caught her in the act and took the little reading lamp away.

"There was a glow," her mother would say. Or, "I saw some light coming through the cracks."

Now Hillary trained her eyes on the window and looked for cracks. She ran her eyes across the whole expanse of Sara-Kate's house and watched for glows. She came to the hedge and squeezed through just far enough for a clear view.

The house was as gray and unrevealing as the face of a cliff. Windows pocked the dark surface at regular intervals, but there was no sense of depth behind them. They were like unimportant chinks in a block of stone. In fact, it was the weight of Sara-Kate's house that Hillary felt more than any other thing at that moment, as if the place really were made of rock so dense that it had tipped the land it stood on. Down, down, it plunged into the black trough of Sara-Kate's yard, while behind Hillary, her own house was lifted up, bright and light as a feather, toward the starry sky.

Hillary shook her head and sighed. Her father must have been wrong. The Connollys' house was as deserted as it had been these past two weeks. In a way, she was relieved. Now she could climb the slope of her own yard, slip back inside her own house, and go to bed without anyone ever guessing she had been away. And tomorrow, perhaps, the snow would come, enough to go sledding this time. Her mother would make hot chocolate, and her father would tinker with the snow blower, which was always breaking down just when it was needed.

There was a long-standing family joke about it. And who knew? she might invite Alison and Jane to go to a movie with her tomorrow afternoon, or to build an igloo.

A black figure came out of Sara-Kate's house and sat down on the doorstep.

It came so quickly and unobtrusively that Hillary felt no surprise. The door made a tiny sound and then the figure was seated, slim and shadowy, on the step. Hillary leaned forward and held her breath.

Sitting motionless as it was, the figure was all but invisible. If Hillary hadn't seen it move before, she could never have picked it out now against the house. Was it Sara-Kate? Hillary strained her eyes at the shadow. She thought she detected the shape of a head turned away from her. She thought she saw an arm. Or was it a leg? She could see pieces of this shadowy person but she couldn't put it together into a whole.

She whispered, "Sara-Kate?" but so timidly that the name hardly left her lips. The shadow didn't move. Was something really there? Had she imagined it?

Then the shadow moved. It stood up and sauntered out into the yard. It was small, and thin as wire, and it was not wearing a coat. A dry crunching sound came from under its feet, which seemed heavier and bulkier than the rest. With its hands in its pockets, the shadow ambled across the yard toward the elf village. It made a wispy noise as if expelling breath. It bent over briefly to look at something, then righted itself. It moved on toward the fallen Ferris wheel.

"Sara-Kate!"

Hillary stepped from the bushes as she said the name a second time. But once in the open, she stopped.

"Hillary?" The shadow turned with what seemed to be a hint of eagerness.

"Sara-Kate? I wasn't sure it was you."

"Of course it's me. Who else would be walking around in my yard in the dark?" Sara-Kate leaned over and picked up the Ferris wheel.

Hillary approached her warily. The figure in front of her looked like Sara-Kate and talked like Sara-Kate, but something made Hillary hang back.

"I thought you were gone," she said. "I thought you moved away. You were never at school. You were never here."

"I was gone," Sara-Kate said. "But now I'm back. For a little while, anyway." She regarded Hillary through the complicated wires of the Ferris wheel she was holding up for examination. "It's not broken," she said about the wheel. "It can work again. Maybe you should come over tomorrow and help me clean up this mess." She waved her hand around the yard, ending up with the battered elf village.

Hillary followed the arc of that wonderful sweep of hand with hungry eyes. She wanted to come more than anything. She wanted to fling her arms around Sara-Kate's thin shoulders and hug her. But still she was suspicious.

"It's supposed to snow tomorrow," she said. "I don't know if I can come." She looked Sara-Kate in the eye and added, "The elves are back, too, aren't they?"

"Yes," Sara-Kate said. Hillary glanced away. She didn't need to be told what she could already feel. All around her, the yard was starting up again. She heard a faint humming noise coming from the overturned washing machine. She heard an infinitesimal clicking in the dead grasses, a rustle among the bushes.

Sara-Kate had leaned over to lift the Ferris wheel back onto its two cinder blocks. She centered the great wheel upon the metal rod and straightened some wires that had bent under the impact of the fall. When they were fixed, she stepped away to admire her work from a distance.

"Watch!" Sara-Kate commanded. Her hand swept the air again. Directly overhead came the sharp cry of a bird. It seemed impossible on this wintry night, with the temperature steadily dropping and a storm on the way, but there it was.

And then, more impossible still, the Ferris wheel began to turn. Slowly, haltingly, as if pushed by invisible hands, it moved around, once, twice. It picked up speed and started a more methodical spin. Though there had seemed to be little light in Sara-Kate's dark yard, the wheel's spokes were illuminated. They flickered past Hillary's eyes, faster and faster, until the wires and spokes were spun together into a silvery tapestry, and the Popsicle-stick seats flew out like golden rockets from the rim.

Then silently, by degrees, the Ferris wheel slowed. The wires became visible again. The Popsicle sticks drew in. The spokes separated themselves, and the big wheel wound down, darkened, and finally stopped.

Up above, wind churned the leafless branches of the trees, then blew past. Hillary blinked.

"Now will you come tomorrow?" Sara-Kate demanded in her ear.

Hillary nodded. She couldn't take her eyes off the wheel.

"Was it the elves who made it spin?" she asked. "It was the elves, wasn't it? But, for a minute, it looked as if . . ."

She turned in wonder to the thin figure beside her.

"Sh-sh-sh," whispered Sara-Kate. She beamed her tiny eyes on Hillary. "It's better not to talk about it."

Ten

How Hillary, in her excited state, got back inside her house, out of her coat, and upstairs to bed without her parents seeing, she hardly knew. She nearly ran into her father coming up the cellar stairs, muttering to himself. But she dodged into the kitchen and he passed on to the bathroom, which gave her time to race up the front stairway and into her room.

It was ten o'clock exactly and she had just slipped under the covers when her mother looked in sleepily to see if she was still awake.

"What an independent child you are," Mrs. Lenox said, coming over to give Hillary a hug. "What did you do all evening? I never heard a sound, and now you've even put yourself to bed. You won't need a mother at all by next year. I'd better start interviewing for a new position."

"Silly," Hillary said, smiling up at her. "I'll always need a mother." But she offered not a word of explanation, and after her mother had gone she lay awake thinking wild and dazzling thoughts that made her feel quite separate from her parents and their ordinary lives.

For Hillary had seen an elf that night. She was sure of it. To lie still in bed and think everything through only made it clearer. All those days of peering into bushes, all those afternoons imagining faces in the leaves seemed ridiculous now when the real thing had been walking around in plain view the whole time.

How stupid she had been to suppose that elves must have pointed feet and little caps. How idiotic to think they must always be tiny. These ideas were held by a world that knew nothing about elves, by people who had never really looked, who were afraid to look, maybe, Hillary thought, remembering how she had pushed Sara-Kate's appearance in the upstairs room from her mind because it seemed so strange and frightening. Not that seeing an elf was easy even when you did want to look. Hillary had been looking at Sara-Kate Connolly for two solid months and only tonight had she finally begun to see.

Sara-Kate had thick skin not because she was "like an elf" but because she was one. Sara-Kate wasn't miniature or green but she had the elf's thin body and the elfin quickness. ("I'd never seen a person that small run so fast," Hillary's father had said.)

Sara-Kate ate elf foods like berries and mint leaves. She hid herself inside the sagging folds of her old clothes in the same way the elves hid within the junk and disorder of the Connollys' backyard. And how had she come to know so much about elves in the first place except by knowing them from the inside, by being one?

The elves in Sara-Kate's yard had not come to

live there by chance, Hillary now saw. Sara-Kate hadn't simply found them one day outside her back door as she pretended. The elves were there because Sara-Kate was there. She was their leader and protector. She kept their small community safe from the outside world. When Sara-Kate went away, the elves went with her. And when the weather grew too cold for even the thickness of an elf, she brought the precious magic beings inside to live in her empty house—an elf house, it must be—with her strangely sick mother.

Hillary lay in her bed shivering with the force of these thoughts. It seemed that her mind had become ten times sharper, ten times brighter, and that it could go into dark places that had confounded it before. Such was the energy of her imagination, that she wondered if she were becoming a bit of an elf herself. Was it possible to become an elf by associating with one?

Hillary stayed awake for hours that night. When she slept at last, she entered dreams that were filled with magic and the impossible possibilities of things, dreams that, oddly enough, were not so different from what was happening to her in her real waking life at that moment.

Hillary woke the next morning to a world in silent frenzy outside her window. Armies of snowflakes swirled before her eyes. The round outline of her father's garden was already erased and the birdbath had collected an odd-looking drift on top. It rose in the basin like a lop-sided white flame, giving the birdbath the unexpected look of an Olympic torch.

"A foot of snow fallen and another foot predicted," Mrs. Lenox informed Hillary when she arrived in the kitchen for breakfast. School was cancelled and "The snow blower's broken, of course," her mother said.

"Of course," Hillary replied.

"See that white mound crawling on its knees out there on what used to be our driveway?" her mother went on, gesturing out the window.

Hillary nodded.

"That's your father. He's dropped the screwdriver."

However, this snowstorm, like many of its relatives, had no intention of being cast in the role of predictable, and shortly after ten o'clock it tapered off to a sprinkle, then stopped. The sky cleared. The air warmed. Sara-Kate's house, which had been hidden all morning behind curtains of falling snow, came into view before Hillary's anxious eyes. She'd been half afraid the place would vanish during the storm, whisking Sara-Kate from her grasp again.

She was out the door tramping eagerly toward the Connollys' yard before her father had finished plowing the front walk. But then, seeing that Sara-Kate was not yet there, she hung back by the hedge. After all that had happened, she felt shy about entering without an invitation. The snow rose over her knees in places and had changed the appearance of everything. It lay in an unblemished white blanket over the yard, concealing all but the trees and the largest bushes, and giving the open spaces a virtuous, barren look.

The rusty washing machine had become a gentle rise and fall in this soft-rolling landscape. The piles of car parts, the tires, the glass, the rotten wood and tin cans were smoothed away. The house itself looked more respectable surrounded by such tidiness and dressed in snow garlands along its gutters and windowsills. And finally, as if these gifts of cleanliness and order were not enough, the sun came out suddenly from behind the last snow cloud and hurled a dazzling light upon it all.

Hillary stepped back into the shade of the hedge and hooded her eyes with one hand. She was not impressed by the snow's transforming powers. Where, she wondered, was the elf village? Had it suffocated under all this heavy beauty?

While the yard shone with the brilliance of diamonds, Hillary's thoughts plunged like moles under the snow to the dirty, junky places she knew and trusted. And she had just about figured out where the Ferris wheel stood, invisible though it was, and the approximate location of the little houses, when Sara-Kate emerged and issued the invitation she'd been waiting for.

"Why are you standing there staring like an idiot?" Sara-Kate yelled in a most irritating and un-elf-like voice. "Come on. Let's get started!"

These words set what was to be the disconcertingly ordinary tone of the morning, for not once did Sara-Kate reveal a flicker of elf-ness. Though Hillary longed for another sign, though she dropped hints about "elf magic" and finally asked Sara-Kate point blank if the Ferris wheel would spin again, the thin girl did not respond. She pretended to have forgotten everything about the night before. It was a great disappointment until Hillary reflected how "elf-like" even this behavior was. How could Sara-Kate be expected to cast her invisibleness aside all at once? Naturally she would find it safer to appear and disappear like her smaller relatives, to show only parts of herself until Hillary had proven trustworthy.

"Which I will," Hillary murmured with determination. "I will."

After this, Hillary stopped looking for signs. And indeed, Sara-Kate continued to play her role so convincingly that the whole issue began to seem rather silly in the light of the day, so snowy and free from school. And there was so much to be done! The village had literally to be excavated, house by house, stone by stone, like the ruins of Pompeii. Everything was there somewhere, but where? And how were they to find it without stepping on it first?

They divided the area into four sections and worked each section carefully and thoroughly in turn. Once a house was discovered, the gentlest fingers were needed to free it from the snow. This was slow work. Even Sara-Kate's hands turned numb and achy and had to be thawed out with warm breath, and then held in her pockets for a while.

After a house was unearthed, its yard could be dug out more quickly with mittened hands. Sara-Kate borrowed one of Hillary's mittens. But the stones in the little stone walls were always getting in the way and being knocked around.

"Let's just put them in a pile for now. Then we can lay them down in the right places when the whole village is cleared out," Sara-Kate suggested. "Also, all these leaf roofs have fallen apart and I was thinking that the elves might like wooden ones instead. There's a pile of wooden shingles under the back steps. Shall I get them out?"

Hillary nodded. She was working on a different problem.

"According to our calculations, the water well should be right about here," she said, pointing to a patch of snow she had been probing with a stick. "But, it's not. What could've happened?"

They found out a moment later when Sara-Kate stepped back from the house she had been working on. A muffled crunch came from under her boot.

"Oh, no!"

"It's a house!" cried Hillary, rushing over to look.

"But how could it be? There aren't supposed to be any here."

"And here's another!" exclaimed Hillary, just saving herself from putting her own foot on it.

Sara-Kate looked thoroughly alarmed.

"Wait a minute!" she said angrily. "Has somebody been building more elf houses in this yard while I wasn't here?" She gazed at Hillary, who shook her head.

"Then how could . . ."

"I know what it is," Hillary said. "We've figured the village out wrong, that's all. Look, the rest of the houses lie under the snow in this direction, not up there where we were looking for the well. And that means the well must really be just . . . about . . . here." She probed a patch of snow and nodded at Sara-Kate.

"It's here," she confirmed.

Sara-Kate seemed relieved.

"Whew!" she said. "I thought maybe these houses were multiplying by themselves during the night."

"Well, I suppose there's nothing to keep an elf from building more houses if she needs them, is there?" Hillary couldn't help saying. She sent one more meaningful look in Sara-Kate's direction but the older girl took no notice. She put her head down and started excavating the house she had stepped on. For the next half hour, no one spoke as the laborious work continued.

At last, however, the village began to emerge again. On all sides, dramatic peaks of snow towered over the little houses as a result of snow-removal operations. The peaks gave the village the cozy look of a hamlet nestled in the foothills of the mountains, though what the serious-minded elves would think of this, Hillary was not sure. Certainly, they would have more difficulty coming and going over the snowy terrain. Would they provide themselves with cross-country skis?

Hillary smiled at this thought. She was about to ask Sara-Kate for her views on the matter when she noticed her standing rigidly beyond the village, her face turned toward her house. She was looking at the window on the second floor, Hillary saw. Its shade had been drawn up. Some commotion was underway up there, a silent flutter behind the glass.

Hillary stepped forward and caught sight of Sara-Kate's face. It was as tense as a knotted fist, wholly absorbed in the action above.

Hillary took another step forward.

"Is it your mother?" she asked softly.

"Yes."

"Is she still sick?"

"Yes." Sara-Kate stared up at the window. "She wants me to come in." She sounded tired.

"It's all right. Do you want me to go home?" Hillary asked her.

"I guess so."

"All right."

Sara-Kate sighed and turned to look at Hillary. There, in Hillary's face, she seemed to see something that interested her, something new and rather amazing if her expression told the truth.

Sara-Kate blinked. She folded her thin arms across her chest and examined the younger girl again.

"What is it?" Hillary said. She felt that she was

standing in a spotlight. "Do you want me to do something?"

Sara-Kate looked at her. "My mother has been worse lately and she likes to have me stay near her," she said. "Do you have any money?"

"I could get some," Hillary said.

Sara-Kate stared at her.

"Without telling anyone," Hillary added quickly.

"We are out of things," Sara-Kate told her. "My mother likes coffee and milk. And sugar. We need bread and some kind of fruit. She likes fruit."

A moment of silence rose between them. Hillary glanced up at the window over their heads, but she couldn't see anything. She looked back at Sara-Kate.

"What else?" she asked the small, tense figure before her.

"Whatever." Sara-Kate shrugged. "Anything. It doesn't matter."

"Should I go to the store?" Hillary asked.

"Yes."

"Should I go right now?"

"Yes," Sara-Kate said. "If you can get some money."

Without another word, Hillary turned and began to go home. She walked steadily, in a dignified way, until she reached the hedge. Once through it, though, out of sight of Sara-Kate, she started to run.

Eleven ✗

Not even in her wildest dreams would Hillary have done the things she now did if Sara-Kate had not asked her. Never would she have thought of doing them or, after planning, have carried them out with such a cold, clear mind.

In the next hour she would lie to her mother, she would steal twice, she would walk alone down forbidden streets, and transact business in a grocery store with the composure of an adult.

"It was no trouble at all," she would tell Sara-Kate afterwards, handing over the bag of groceries in the Connollys' kitchen. It was almost the truth. Hillary had never been so proud to be trusted with a mission in her life.

"What did you tell your mother?"

"I didn't tell her anything. She was upstairs. I took a ten-dollar bill from her wallet on the counter. Then I called up to her and said you'd invited me for lunch."

Sara-Kate grinned. "That must have surprised her."

"It did."

She'd run out the kitchen door before her mother could protest. She'd gone through the hedge into Sara-Kate's yard, then around the house to the street in front. Most sidewalks weren't shoveled yet so she'd walked on the slushy side of the road. She knew the way from her trips with Sara-Kate and she wasn't afraid, not even when a car honked at her for being too far out from the curb.

In fact, she'd felt the opposite of fear: a slow-rising excitement. The day was so bright, the snow was so deep. There was a lawlessness in the air, a sense of regular rules not applying, of their being cancelled, like school. Cars nosed along the streets in a bumbling way, avoiding drifts and stranded vehicles. Children waded like penguins through gleaming white yards, or built snow forts, or sucked on porch icicles. Office workers who should have been at their desks hours ago shoveled their driveways lazily and talked to their neighbors. It was all so breathtaking, so free and easy, that Hillary wanted to kick up her heels and turn cartwheels in the street. But she kept herself on course, kept her face blank. She knew that she was more lawless than anything in that day and must not draw attention to herself.

"That will be $13.05 please."

"$13.05!" Hillary looked into the unsmiling face of the man behind the cash register. "But I only have ten dollars."

"Then you'll have to put something back."

"But, I can't! I promised I'd . . ."

The man sighed, rolled his eyes, and leaned toward her over the counter.

"I guess it'll have to be the bologna," Hillary said quickly.

She hated to give it up, though. The bologna was Hillary's idea of something extra that Mrs. Connolly might like. Meat was good for you. It made you strong. She'd retraced her steps to the cold-cuts case to put the package back but in the end the place she put it was in her pocket.

"Lucky the pockets in this jacket are big," she said to Sara-Kate in the kitchen, though she still quaked inside to think of what she had done.

Sara-Kate glanced at her. "You have to be careful of the mirrors," she said. "They have mirrors high up in the corners that can show what you're doing."

It was her way of saying thank you, and Hillary answered with a nod. She knew they were speaking a special language now, and more than that, that she had passed a test and been ushered through a secret door. Next, Sara-Kate asked, rather formally because they were coming together so fast: "Please stay. I'll be right back."

She took the paper bag and went upstairs. The electric stove in the middle of the room had been turned on. Faint waves of heat came across the cold floor from the oven's mouth. Hillary walked over and sat in one of the armchairs in the strange room-within-a-room. Now she could see why it was arranged as it was. The old stove wasn't powerful enough to heat the whole room, but if you stayed near it, you could be warm. The fan on the stove was working. It blew the heat toward her in a soft, pleasant way, as it was intended to do, she guessed.

Hillary took off her boots. They were wet inside from her hike through the snow. She sat back in the chair. She leaned her head against the chair's padded interior and thought how exciting it was to be here, on this most unusual island in the midst of the everyday world. All around the Connollys' house, the town honked and bumped, clanked and thudded, without an inkling of the secrets held within. It gave Hillary a delicious feeling to be sitting in such a private place, to have come through the ordinary face of things into Sara-Kate's hidden world. She stretched her hands out toward the oven's warmth and waited for her friend to come back.

In a little while, she heard the tread of boots on the stairs. Then Sara-Kate appeared, still carrying the paper bag.

"Is your mother all right?" Hillary asked, jumping up.

Sara-Kate shrugged. "She's okay. She says you really can stay for lunch, if you want to that is." Her eyes skirted Hillary's.

"Want to? I'd *love* to!" Hillary said. "Do you know that you've never invited me in before? Not once. I mean the last time I was here it wasn't really . . . well, I just came by accident. I wasn't spying on you, honest," she ended quickly. Sara-Kate had given her a look.

"It's all right," the older girl replied. "I know you didn't tell."

"I wouldn't have even gone upstairs except that I

thought the elves were there," Hillary explained.

"Elves in this house?" Sara-Kate produced an explosive hoot.

"Well, I was sure they were, and I still think—"

"Hey!" Sara-Kate cut in. "We're wasting time. Let's have a party. Come on! We've got everything." Then, in one of her wild leaps of mood, she began to race around the inner room, snatching a knife from a drawer slot, tossing the bag in the air, dumping its contents on the stove top.

"Bologna sandwiches!" cried Sara-Kate. She trumpeted through her fists. "Toodle-tee-toot-tee-too. Charge! That's what they do at the football games at the high school," she said to Hillary. "I go over and watch on Saturdays when I feel like it. It's neat. Do you want to come next time?"

"The high school is way across town!" Hillary protested.

Sara-Kate didn't hear. She was blowing more blasts on her trumpet and charging into the making of the sandwiches. Two slices of bread down flat, slap, then a thick stack of bologna slices on top of each one, slap, slap, and more bread on top of that, slap, no mayonnaise, no lettuce, no mustard. So what?

"I'd like to go see a football game," Hillary had to admit in the middle of the slappings and trumpetings. "In fact I guess I'd love to."

They sat side by side on the ragged, falling-apart chairs. Sara-Kate devoured her sandwich like a lion.

Hillary took polite bites and chewed thoroughly, as she'd been taught at home.

"Want another one?" Sara-Kate was up and flying again before Hillary had finished her third bite. She grabbed two mugs from the shelves in the drawerless bureau and filled them to the very top with milk.

"Watch out!" cried Hillary. "They're spilling."

Sara-Kate giggled. "Would you like to see how Pierre the Package drinks out of a cup?"

"Who's he?"

"He's awful," Sara-Kate whispered. She rolled her tiny eyes. "He's horrible. I read about him in one of those newspapers they sell in the bus station. See, he's got no arms or legs. Just a little stump for a body. It's all wrapped up in cloth, like a package. Anyway, here he is drinking."

She lowered her lips to the rim of a cup and, with her arms bent at a painful-looking angle behind her back, slurped at the milk.

"Want me to do your cup, too?" she asked, looking around.

"Ugh. Okay."

"Pierre the Package had to learn to do everything with his mouth," Sara-Kate went on, more seriously, when she had finished slurping Hillary's milk.

"Don't tell me," said Hillary. "I don't want to know."

"He types letters to people by holding a stick in his mouth to hit the typewriter keys. He turns on lamps and faucets with his teeth. He makes sand-

wiches and feeds his dog. Yup, he has a dog, a cute little terrier that jumps up in his wheelchair and licks the mess off his face after dinner. And listen to this. The way Pierre reads a book is by flicking the pages over with his tongue."

"Ugh! Ugh!" Hillary covered her own mouth with her hands, a thing Pierre the Package wouldn't be able to do no matter how disgusted he felt, she thought suddenly.

"We should try reading that way sometime," Sara-Kate was saying. "Who knows when it might come in handy. You know, you can learn to do practically anything if you really want to hard enough."

"Sure, let's try it," Hillary murmured, while Sara-Kate tore into another bologna sandwich and poured herself another mug of milk.

"This is the greatest," Sara-Kate said, leaning back with the mug in one hand. "Isn't this the greatest party? Are you having a good time? See, it's not as bad in this house as you probably thought it would be."

"Bad?" Hillary said.

"I mean, I do okay here as long as they don't switch off the electricity. I try to keep that bill paid up. I used to get heat from a furnace like everybody else, but it broke. It takes big bucks to fix something like that. Upstairs I've got three good electric heaters. Usually I move us up there in the worst weather. Nothing much works down here when it gets really cold."

Hillary stared at the lean planes of Sara-Kate's

face and noticed for the first time the odd little dark marks under her eyes, like tired smudges in a grown-up face.

"One good thing is I've got two of these hot plates so I don't have to haul them up and down stairs," the elf-girl went on. "Wherever I happen to be when I want to cook, I can cook." She smiled. "I bet you don't have that in your house."

"No, we don't," Hillary said.

"And you don't have a big, friendly stove like this that you can lie back with and put your feet up on."

"No."

Sara-Kate stuck her work boots up on the stove and stretched out luxuriously in her chair. "And you can't have parties like this either, with just two people or whoever you want to invite, and whatever you want to eat. Are you still hungry? How about a cup of coffee? Whenever you've got a space left you can always fill it up with coffee."

Hillary leaned toward her suddenly. She put her hand on Sara-Kate's arm and said: "You do everything around here, don't you? You run this whole house."

Sara-Kate sat up. "What do you mean?" she asked, on guard in an instant.

"You keep pretending that your mother is the one telling you what to do, like everyone else's mother. But that's not right, is it? She doesn't tell you anything. She's too sick. You're the one taking care of her."

"That's not true!" Sara-Kate replied. "My mother

does tell me what to do. She tells me things all the time."

"But you're the one who does everything in the end," Hillary went on. "You buy all the food and do all the cooking."

"So what?"

"You pay the bills and wash the clothes and when something breaks, like the furnace, you decide what to do about it."

"So what?" Sara-Kate spat at her. "I learned how. I can do it. I help my mother, that's all. I bet even you have to help your stupid mother sometimes."

Hillary didn't get angry. She looked at Sara-Kate hard, as if she were trying to bring her into focus. "It's all right," she said. "I would never tell anybody. I was just imagining how it would be. What happens if there's something only your mother can do, like sign something, or talk on the phone? What if she needs to go somewhere, to the doctor or the hair-dresser?"

At that, Sara-Kate sagged in her chair. She sighed. She looked at Hillary as if she were two years old instead of nine, and folded her arms across her chest in that all-knowing, impatient attitude so character-istic of her.

"Look, whatever happens, I fix it," she told Hillary. "I sign it if it needs to be signed. I write it if it needs to be written. I learned my mother's writing. I talk on the phone, too, when it's working. I tell people what to do and they do it. Or, if they don't, I find some other way. I'm good at things like that.

My mother used to get upset all the time. Her mind's not always right, so then she gets sick. See, sometimes the envelope comes and sometimes it doesn't come. I learned what to do when it doesn't come."

"What envelope?" Hillary asked.

"You know, with the check, the money," Sara-Kate answered. "A lot of times, my father can't send it. He's not exactly rich. So then we run out."

"Run out! But then what do you do?" Hillary said, appalled. "How do you buy things like food and . . ." Her hands were rising up to her mouth again. She was looking at Sara-Kate over the top of them. "Like food and . . ." She couldn't think, suddenly, of all the things that Sara-Kate would need to buy. All the hundreds of things. "Like food and, you know," she ended lamely.

Sara-Kate shrugged. "I know," she said.

Twelve ✗

The afternoon was passing. Through the torn shade of the window over the sink, Hillary detected the sun's shifted position. It was no longer overhead, hot and bright, but lower in the sky, half-screened by trees and neighboring houses. She thought that she ought to be going home soon. Her mother would begin to wonder where she was. She might be looking out the Lenoxes' dining-room window at this very minute, peering down at Sara-Kate's shadowy house: *Where is my child?*

Well, I'm here. Don't worry, Hillary answered her mother in her mind. I'm inside where I wanted to be, with Sara-Kate. And we're having a party in the magic inner room. At least I think it's a party.

Hillary gazed about herself and wondered suddenly if "magic" was quite the right word for this place, which now looked rather grim with the sun at its new angle. There was a hole in the floor near the sink, she noticed. Beside her, Sara-Kate was flipping her hair carelessly over her shoulder, preparing to answer the question about the envelope that didn't come, the money that ran out.

"So what *do* you do?" Hillary asked her again. She was met by yet another of Sara-Kate's weary shrugs.

"I get by. I know some ways."

"What ways?"

"People are always leaving their stuff around in a town like this. There was a whole shopping cart of food in the supermarket parking lot one time. At school there's lost and found. I could wear all designer clothes if I wanted. I don't take that kind of stuff, though. Who wants to look like those dumb show-offs?"

Hillary nodded.

"Hey, I should show you how to get into the movies for free sometime!" Sara-Kate exclaimed. "It's really easy. I'm not always broke, you know, but I never pay for the movies because it would be a waste. We should do it together. You'd see."

"What happens if you get caught?" Hillary asked uneasily.

"Who gets caught?" Sara-Kate's small eyes skimmed over her. "I bet you think I'm dumb because I got put back in school. That's what a lot of people think, and it's too bad for them. Just when they've decided how dumb I am and how smart they are, right then is when they happen to lose something. Something of theirs just disappears out the window."

Perhaps the sun had settled another inch. A finger of cold air caught the back of Hillary's neck and she shivered.

"You shouldn't do that," she said to Sara-Kate. "It's not right at all. You should ask someone for help instead of stealing all the time. If people knew you were living here taking care of your mother by yourself, they'd have to do something about it. They'd have to—"

"Wreck everything! That's right," Sara-Kate interrupted with a flash of anger. "Nobody knows how to take care of my mother except me. They've tried to do it. Even my father tried, but he couldn't so he left. Now I'm doing it. I've done it for a year so far and nobody even knows. People are stupid. They can't see a thing. They don't have a clue to what's going on right under their noses, in their own backyards."

Hillary stared at her.

"Do you know what would happen if I called somebody up on the phone and asked for help? Do you know what they would do?" Sara-Kate stood before Hillary with her hands on her hips and the whole rest of her body moving—twisting, jumping, quivering, kicking. It made Hillary think of the elf in her, the strange elf-ness that came at certain moments and then hid away again, came and went, so that Hillary could never finally decide who this small, fierce person was. She could never decide if she was cruel or warm-hearted, magic or ordinary, thick-skinned or fragile, a friend or a fraud.

"They would take my mother away," Sara-Kate said, without waiting for Hillary to decide this time either. Her voice had dropped to a whisper.

"But why?" Hillary asked. "Where would they take her?"

"They would put her someplace far away, out of sight."

"But why?"

"Listen Hillary, regular people don't like us, that's why. They don't like other people who live different from them, other people who are sick. They don't want us around. They don't want to look."

"Don't want to look!"

"So if you're thinking of going somewhere and getting help for us, don't do it. The only help we'd get is the kind that would look away and shake its head. Then it'd grab us by the neck and drag us off someplace we didn't want to go."

"But . . ."

"Help is the last thing you want to ask for when you're somebody like me," Sara-Kate told Hillary. "People like you can ask for help. People like me have to steal it."

Sara-Kate sat down abruptly in the other ragged chair. She sat without looking, knowing exactly, to the inch, where it was behind her. She knew everything about this crazy room-within-a-room because she had made it herself, Hillary understood. She was the one who had turned the drawers into tables, the bureau into shelves. She had positioned the fan on the stove to spread the heat around. She had organized everything, figured out everything, pushed everything together and forced it to work. And she had done it by herself. No one had told her, "Do it." No one had explained, "This is the only way." She was all by herself, separate from the world. She was her own single, strong, secret person.

Hillary moved toward her. "Are you an elf?" she asked Sara-Kate, who brought her head up with a jerk. "An elf," the younger girl repeated, longingly. "You can say it if you are. I'd never tell, I swear. I'll help you with your mother. I'll do anything you say."

Sara-Kate's little eyes had opened wider than Hillary had ever seen them. They looked surprised and puzzled, eager but undecided, and clearly Sara-Kate had something to say. She moistened her lips with her tongue. She pushed her hair off her forehead with the flat of one hand. She kept her eyes trustingly on Hillary and, in a minute no doubt, she would have spoken. She would have explained everything, allowed it to fall into Hillary's lap like a special present, the kind of present that is so precious one is tempted to keep it and not give it to anyone. But Sara-Kate was ready to give, Hillary knew. She was ready to tell at last and they were both leaning forward in their chairs, beginning to smile at each other, when the interruption came. It was a muffled shout:

"Hillary, are you here?"

And then again, from outside, while Hillary and Sara-Kate continued to stare at each other but with changing expressions: "Hillary! Hill . . . a . . . ry!"

"It's my mother. She's in the yard." Hillary jumped out of her chair.

Sara-Kate leapt up, too. "Go and meet her, quick. Keep her away. She can't come in here."

"Where's my coat?" Hillary wailed. She looked around wildly.

"Hurry up! Get going!" Sara-Kate's hands had rolled themselves into fists. "She's coming to the door. I can hear her coming!"

Hillary found her coat on the floor between the chairs. She stuffed her feet into her boots and ran for the door.

"I'll come back later," was all she had time to whisper. Sara-Kate was waving her away frantically.

"Go on! Go on!"

"Hillary? Are you in there?" Mrs. Lenox's unmistakable voice came through the door, followed by the sound of knocking.

Thirteen ✗

It seemed so odd to be answering the knock of her own mother, to be opening a door that neither had met through before, that Hillary hardly knew what to say when Mrs. Lenox's familiar face appeared across the threshold.

"Good heavens! Here you are," her mother exclaimed. "I've been calling and calling. You've been here for hours. I really do think it's time to come home."

She gazed anxiously at Hillary, then looked past her into the room beyond.

"Goodbye and thank you!" Hillary cried loudly, on cue. She gave the door a yank to pull it closed, but it struck the side of her boot and bounced open wider than ever.

"Good heavens!" Mrs. Lenox said again, looking through the opening. "Is that you, Sara-Kate?"

Sara-Kate said nothing. She stood as if frozen against the side of the white stove in the inner room.

"What's going on here?" Mrs. Lenox asked, in a more determined tone. "What's happened to this room?"

"It's nothing!" Hillary cried. "It's just Sara-Kate. Come on, let's go!"

"Wait a minute," Mrs. Lenox said, with an ominous note of concern in her voice. She stepped around Hillary and through the door.

"This place looks like some kind of fort," she said, addressing Sara-Kate. "What have you been doing? Where is your mother?"

There was a moment's pause, just long enough for a single, swift intake of breath. Then Sara-Kate moved forward with a practiced, gliding motion. Her tiny eyes zeroed in on Hillary's mother and her face composed itself into a mask of perfect politeness, an expression that Hillary had never seen on it before. Sara-Kate met Mrs. Lenox halfway across the room. She shook her hand in a most courteous and charming way.

"Hello, Mrs. Lenox. I'm so glad to see you again. I guess it's been a while. My mother is fine, but she's upstairs having a nap. I know this room looks terrible. We're having it fixed up so we had to move everything around. I'm sorry you had to come looking for Hillary."

"I did try to telephone," Hillary's mother put in.

"Well, the phone's been off since this morning, as you probably found out," Sara-Kate said smoothly. Hillary stood to one side, marveling at the ease with which Sara-Kate was inventing.

"It's the snowstorm, I guess," she went on. "There's a man who's coming soon to fix it."

Mrs. Lenox looked around helplessly. Something was wrong, but she could not put her finger on what it was that so alarmed her about the house.

"Is the heat off, too?" she asked. "This room is so cold."

"They had to turn it off, just for an hour or two, so they could work on some pipes," Sara-Kate explained.

" 'They'?"

"You know, the workmen who are fixing up the house," said the thin elf-girl with the ragged wheaten hair. There was just a hint of irritation in her polite voice to let Mrs. Lenox know that she was imposing, that she would do well, now, to stop and go home. Hillary knew that Sara-Kate had put the irritation in on purpose, to trick her mother. It was an ingenious performance.

Nevertheless, Mrs. Lenox had scented something poisonous in the Connollys' house. Perhaps Sara-Kate was a bit too thin. Perhaps her hair was a trifle too ragged. Perhaps it was her boots, after all, that were her undoing. They looked so black and so shabby laced up on the end of her twig-like legs, as if she had stolen them off some drunken bum in the park, which perhaps she had.

"I believe I would like to speak to your mother anyway, if you don't mind," Mrs. Lenox said to Sara-Kate, cutting straight to the middle of things.

"I don't think she wants to be bothered," Sara-Kate replied evenly. "I'll have her give you a call when the telephone's fixed."

"No, thank you." Mrs. Lenox became more polite the more insistent she was. "Now, if you'll just tell her I'm here—or even better, show me where she is," Mrs. Lenox said, for she had seen a strange light flash in Sara-Kate's eyes.

"Please go away," said the thin girl. She stood directly in front of Hillary's mother.

"I don't know what you think you're up to," Mrs. Lenox said angrily, "but I am now going to speak to your mother."

"Mother!" Hillary cried. "Please don't! Please come!" She tried to pull her back by the arm, but how can a child pull an angry grown-up away from something she is determined to do? Mrs. Lenox walked forward despite the arms dragging her back, and the body blocking her.

Hillary let go when she saw how strong her mother was. She looked at Sara-Kate to see what she would do next. She hoped Sara-Kate had something up her sleeve, some further trick for escaping this predicament. If ever there was a need for magic, it was now. Mrs. Lenox walked across the Connollys' empty dining room, glancing around as though she had landed on an alien planet.

Hillary waited for the bird's sharp cry. She waited for a blast of wind, a streak of light, for an elf's miracle. Nothing happened. Her mother entered the front hall.

"What are you going to do?" Hillary whispered to Sara-Kate as her mother began to climb the stairs. Sara-Kate seemed not to hear. She pushed her hair out of her eyes with one hand.

"Sara-Kate! Do something! She's going to find out," Hillary cried when Mrs. Lenox turned left at the top of the staircase. They were standing side by side at the bottom, and Sara-Kate didn't answer. She stared toward the second floor.

Hillary heard the sound of a door opening up above. Then she heard her mother's voice:

"Good heavens! May I come in? I'm Helen Lenox from up the hill. Is everything all right?"

Sara-Kate turned her face slowly toward Hillary. She beamed her two tiny eyes straight into Hillary's eyes for one flash of a moment. Then she turned herself around and sat down on the bottom step.

"Don't be afraid," Hillary heard her mother saying gently in the second-floor room. "Don't be frightened. I'm here to help."

Fourteen ✗

Sitting on that stair was how Hillary last saw Sara-Kate Connolly "in person" as she later thought of it. It was the last chance she had to say anything to Sara-Kate. But right then was when it was least possible to say anything, so there were no final questions, no good-byes.

Upstairs, Hillary's mother was speaking to Sara-Kate's mother in quiet, grown-up tones, and raising shades to let in the winter sun. Downstairs, Sara-Kate sat silent on the step, and even if one could believe that there were elves in the world, and that she once had been one, Hillary saw there was no magic in her now. There was no thick skin and no uncanny quickness. She was the same frightened child that any child would be whose family was in trouble. She was waiting on the step the way every child would wait to see what would happen next, what the grown-ups would decide.

Hillary's legs felt shaky, so she turned and sat beside Sara-Kate on the stairs, and they were so much the same size that their shoulders met exactly. Their bent knees rose to the same height. Their arms lay side by side in the same angles and attitudes. There Mrs. Lenox found them when she came back

· 105

downstairs. She leaned over the girls and hugged them both at once. She told them everything would be all right now. She was going to get help.

Mrs. Lenox told Sara-Kate to stay with her mother until she came back with the help, and she told Hillary to come home with her, please. So Hillary got up and looked down at Sara-Kate.

"I'm sorry," she whispered, but Sara-Kate turned her face to the wall. Then Mrs. Lenox drew Hillary gently away and they walked toward the back door together.

Never again would Hillary see a house change as fast as the Connollys' house did in the days that followed. Almost from the hour of "the awful discovery," as people were soon describing the event, the place was transformed. Where it had been silent and empty, now it rang with noise: the clatter of feet, the chatter of voices, the snap of shades being raised. Where it had been dark, it was lit up like a stage. The house had been nearly invisible before, unnoticed in its drab and boring decay. Now the eyes of the neighborhood were upon it night and day and the smallest movements were cause for comment. Who was going in? What was coming out? Was that a light in the kitchen? Was that a squirrel on the roof?

Strange bits of information floated about. At least they were strange to Hillary, who, having lately been at the center of the Connollys' world now listened like a spy at the gossipy edges of groups. She listened to her mother speaking softly on the telephone.

Sara-Kate Connolly was in an orphanage and her mother was crazy.

Mrs. Connolly was in a hospital and Sara-Kate was crazy.

Sara-Kate's father could not be traced and relatives were being sought.

Then: Relatives had been found! They were coming.

Then: The relatives were here! From Michigan or Kansas or Montana. They were taking charge of everything.

"And thank goodness for that!" Mrs. Lenox exclaimed. "Now this town can stop worrying and get back to ordinary life. I've never seen such an array of prying eyes and nosy noses. Do you know that a newspaper reporter came by and tried to interview me this morning?" She put her arm around Hillary's shoulder as if to shield her from such attacks, but Hillary stepped away.

"What's going to happen to Sara-Kate?" she asked.

"I suppose she'll go to live with her relatives, poor thing."

"Poor thing! Sara-Kate isn't poor. She won't go anywhere she doesn't want to, I bet."

"She won't have much choice, I'm afraid," Mrs. Lenox said, smoothing her daughter's hair. "You mustn't worry anymore about either Sara-Kate or her mother. They are getting wonderful care and every sort of attention."

"Is it true that the house is going to be fixed up and sold?"

"You sound so angry! Of course it's true. The family needs the money and what else could they do with a house like that?"

"They could leave it alone and let Sara-Kate keep on taking care of her mother there."

"Hillary, that's ridiculous."

"She was doing okay by herself except for running out of money sometimes. And that wasn't her fault. That was because her father didn't send enough and she didn't dare ask anyone for help. She knew people didn't like her, that they wouldn't care. She was right, too," Hillary told her mother. "You should see what's happening down at her house. They're changing everything as fast as they can. They want to make it look as if Sara-Kate never lived there."

"I wish you'd stop going to the Connollys' house," Mrs. Lenox replied.

"I can't stop," Hillary said. "How can I stop? The elf village is there."

"Elf village! Hillary, after all that's happened I hope you still don't think . . ."

"No. I don't. I don't think anything except that Sara-Kate loved the village and she'd want me to take care of it while she's away," Hillary replied quickly.

She went every day to the Connollys' house and watched and listened to everything that happened.

A repairman came to fix the furnace. A telephone man came to reconnect the phone. The dead insects were swept off the dining-room floor by a gang of housecleaners who also made short work of the dust, the cobwebs, the grime in the bathrooms—none of which were working, they reported. It was a shame and a scandal. So the plumber was called to install new pipes, and the electrician was called to rewire the circuits, and a roof man came to fix a hole in the roof.

"Please be careful where you step," Hillary advised these workmen when they entered the yard. She crouched next to the Ferris wheel and placed an arm around it.

"See those little houses over there? See the pool? See the paths?" She pointed with her free hand. Yes, yes, they saw, grinning and winking like mischievous boys. The electrician cringed playfully:

"Is there something magic that lives here, then?"

"There might be. Who knows?" Hillary answered coldly.

"Should we be afraid of being changed into toads?"

"Only if you step on things," Hillary replied, glaring at him as she was sure Sara-Kate would have done. The plumber's work boots looked shockingly familiar.

🦋 Hillary could stand guard over the elf village but she could not protect Sara-Kate from the things that people continued to say about her. She could not stop the whispered stories, the mean remarks. Even the newspaper, which Hillary had always thought of as an unbiased reporter of hard fact, came out with the oddest article.

"Is this story really about the Connollys?" she asked her mother. "Because Sara-Kate wasn't keeping her mother prisoner the way it says here. She was taking care of her when no one else could. And she was never 'dirty and dressed in rags.' Sara-Kate washed her clothes and her mother's clothes, too. She folded them carefully in the laundromat. I helped. She was always clean and the house didn't 'reek of garbage' either. It was just empty and dusty and strange. I was there. I saw everything."

Mrs. Lenox shook her head. "Are you sure," she asked Hillary, "that you were seeing everything clearly? Or were you just seeing what Sara-Kate told you to see?"

"No. No!" Hillary protested, but even as she spoke old doubts about Sara-Kate sifted into her mind and she found herself shouting to drive them back: "I know what I saw!"

"Well, whatever was going on down there I'm certainly glad I found you when I did," Mrs. Lenox said firmly, "or what would Sara-Kate have dragged you into next? Running her errands around town? Lying and stealing?"

Hillary flushed and lowered her eyes.

"We all feel sorry for Sara-Kate," her mother went on. "She's had a bad time. But have you ever wondered why she chose you for her friend? Why couldn't she have found someone her own age? Are you sure she really cared about you, Hillary? Or were you just someone who was useful to have around?"

"I think she cared about me *and* thought I was useful," Hillary said, with an angry upward glance, though suddenly she wasn't sure at all. She remembered how easily Sara-Kate had lied to her mother in the Connollys' kitchen. She thought of the older girl's secretiveness, her bursts of rage, her unexplained disappearances. Was it possible that she had not seen Sara-Kate clearly?

At school, the newspaper story fueled a new round of rumors and opinions:

Sara-Kate was a sad, misguided creature who'd been caught in circumstances beyond her understanding.

Sara-Kate was a sharp-eyed, street-wise kid who'd steal the coat off your back if you let her near you.

Sara-Kate was a nut. Hadn't she starved her mother half to death and refused to ask for help?

Sara-Kate was going to a reformatory. No, she wasn't. She was going to Kansas on a plane.

"To Kansas?" Hillary murmured in disbelief. She couldn't see what was true and what was not. There was no higher authority announcing, "This is the final truth!" The more Hillary heard about Sara-Kate, the farther away she went. Her small, thin figure was disappearing behind a screen of opinions and facts and newspaper stories, leaving Hillary in a place as dim as the rooms of the Connollys' house.

She was in a land of the unknown and the unknowable, she thought, a black land where not even her parents could help her.

"I am the only one who can decide about Sara-Kate," she whispered to the little elf houses in the Connollys' backyard. "Oh, if she would just come home."

The village comforted her. She kneeled in its midst, repairing roofs, straightening walls, while around her the wonderful yard that had sheltered the tiny community was invaded, laid open to strangers' eyes, littered with the workmen's debris. Its privacy and secrecy evaporated as Hillary watched, and was replaced by the cheapness and indifference of a run-down city park.

"If only Sara-Kate would come out her back door with her usual shout: 'Let's get going!' Then there would be no worry about what to do or what to believe. Then we could start all over again just being friends," Hillary whispered to the village that huddled like a real village at the feet of real snow mountains.

✕ "Is it true that Sara-Kate left yesterday on a plane with her relatives?" Hillary asked her mother one afternoon, after school.

"I think it's true," Mrs. Lenox said, looking up from the potato she was peeling for dinner.

"She never came back to say goodbye. She never called."

"Well, I suppose there wasn't time in the end."

"I think she hates me because I'm the one who got her caught."

"No, no! Of course not! It wasn't your fault. It was no one's fault," Mrs. Lenox cried, running across the kitchen to hug her. But Hillary turned away with tears in her eyes.

Fifteen ✗

In the dark winter days that followed, what Hillary missed most about Sara-Kate, oddly enough, were the very things that had made her so difficult to get along with: her sharp remarks and clear, cold eye. Beside Sara-Kate's crisp manner, beside her quickness and lightness, the girls at school seemed slow and heavy. In fat-faced groups they clumped through the halls, weighted down with fashion clothes and expensive book bags. They pouted and complained, gossiped and giggled, and Hillary watched as if she'd never seen such behavior before, as if she'd never belonged to such a group. She was outside all groups now, but not because she was excluded. Everyone was being rather nice to her, actually.

Her teachers asked after her health. People smiled at her in the halls. Jane and Alison were always putting their arms around her, guiding her toward private nooks where they could whisper together.

"Don't worry if you still feel a little bad about Sara-Kate," Jane said. "She was even worse than we thought, and she got you tied up in complete knots."

"My mother says it would take anyone a little while to get over something like this," Alison added, patting Hillary's hand. "It's not that you were stupid

114 ·

and fell for all the lies Sara-Kate told you, even though you did. It's that Sara-Kate was so terrible. Imagine going to the trouble of cooking up that elf village—"

"Which we finally went over and saw after she left," Jane interrupted. "It's no big deal as far as I'm concerned."

"Me either," Alison said. "And then imagine her making up that whole complicated world of elves, down to the tiniest details of what they like to do and what they like to eat."

"How did you find out about that?" Hillary asked angrily.

"Your mother told our mothers," Jane said. "Don't worry. We understand. We don't blame you at all. It wasn't fair to pick on someone so much younger. We blame Sara-Kate."

"Well, I blame you!" Hillary suddenly found herself yelling at them. "For not understanding one thing that happened. I blame you and I blame everybody in this whole dumb school!"

Not that she understood any better. She didn't. It was what made her so angry at them all, so angry at Sara-Kate, too, when she let herself admit it. If not for the fragile village, which day by day seemed more endangered by the yard, Hillary might have turned her back on everything. She might have walked away up the hill to her own house and shut the door for good.

Why had Sara-Kate left the village behind anyway? she thought crossly. If Sara-Kate cared for it so much, if it was really the magic place she'd pretended, why hadn't she taken it with her, or dismantled it and hidden it in some safer spot? Sara-Kate had gone without a word about the village, as if the place meant nothing and Hillary was nothing, too.

And yet, even as Hillary accused Sara-Kate, another way of looking came into her mind. She had only to approach the village for her bitter arguments to be grasped and whirled around, to be turned inside out by invisible forces. Couldn't it be argued, for instance, that Sara-Kate had left the village behind on purpose? Suppose she had left it as a present for Hillary, or as a sign of friendship. Perhaps it was meant to be a message of sorts, the very message that Hillary longed to receive: "Goodbye. I am all right. I'll stay in touch." To be around the village was certainly to find oneself, willy-nilly, in touch with Sara-Kate. She might no longer be there "in person," but she was there, Hillary discovered.

From her post beside the Ferris wheel, she watched the workmen come and go through the back door that only Sara-Kate had used before. Through the kitchen window, she saw a team of men move the stove back against the wall. How had Sara-Kate ever moved it in the first place? she wondered.

("Elves are strong. And magic," she heard Sara-Kate say in her ear.)

Hillary began to recognize certain real-estate brokers who came to direct house improvements, and she invited herself inside with them to look at the improvements close up: new tile on the kitchen floor; new counter tops; a door for the oven, and new burners. These things were certainly better than the shabby little room-within-a-room that was there before. And yet, there had been something wonderful about that other room, Hillary thought, something in the way the furniture had been taken apart and put together again so strangely. It was as if an entirely different sort of brain were at work behind it.

("Strange and little!" Hillary heard Sara-Kate's angry voice say again. "If you were an elf you wouldn't feel strange or little. You'd feel like a normal, healthy elf.")

A sale of house furniture and goods was announced and a women's group came to polish up the few remaining tables and chairs. Then people arrived to prowl and buy. Hillary prowled with them. She saw Sara-Kate's hot plates being sold, one to a bearded man with a limp, the other to a woman wearing bedroom slippers instead of shoes.

An oriental gentleman with a small and oddly elf-like figure bought the electric fan. He tested it first by lighting matches in its airstream. Then he picked the fan up and shook it like a stubborn catsup bottle. What on earth was he going to use it for? Hillary wondered.

("Why do you think these elves are anything like you?" she heard Sara-Kate ask. "Maybe they're so different that nothing they do is anything like what you do.")

Often on her visits inside the Connollys' house,

Hillary went upstairs and down the hall. She walked into the second-floor room where Sara-Kate and her mother had lived during the very cold weather, where they had hidden when Mrs. Connolly had grown too ill to be left alone and Sara-Kate had stayed with her.

It was empty now, of course. Everything had been taken downstairs to be sold. But those four blank walls still held a glimmer of enchantment for Hillary. She remembered how the door had seemed to bulge with light, how near she had felt to the elves' magic. There were other explanations for the magic, now. There are always other explanations for magic, Hillary thought.

"Sara-Kate was very smart," Mrs. Lenox had explained. "She knew that if she didn't come to school, the school would come looking for her. So she wrote a note withdrawing herself from classes. She used her mother's handwriting and her mother's signature and completely fooled everyone.

"Then, since she had said they were away on a trip, she was careful to keep them both hidden during the day. She didn't answer the door. She kept the shades drawn. The heat was off, of course, because the furnace was broken, and no one could tell they were there at all. At night, Sara-Kate came out under cover of dark while her mother slept. She went for supplies. She must have gone to different stores so as not to be recognized, and of course she didn't always pay for what she took. The night your father saw her she must have been coming home from one of these trips."

"Maybe," Hillary had answered softly. She'd been thinking about Sara-Kate's strange eating habits, about the "delicate stomach" that required hot cereal for school lunch but could suddenly take on large numbers of bologna sandwiches on special occasions. Had Sara-Kate eaten Cream of Wheat because it was the cheapest thing she could get that was hot and filled her up? Perhaps she really didn't like wild berries and mint at all. But then again, maybe she did. Hillary shrugged and glanced at her mother. Perhaps being hungry and cold and angry and alone didn't mean you couldn't still be an elf. In fact, maybe those were exactly the things elves always were, Hillary had thought, as she stood gazing up into her mother's face.

The village looked fragile, but it had staying power. From the window of the second-floor room, Hillary looked down on it, over the new wooden roofs, over the tidy front yards. The Connollys' house brought Sara-Kate back in stray bits and pieces, but the elf village was where she came back all together in Hillary's mind. More and more, the village seemed the only true thing about her, the only fact that was sure.

Here Hillary had first run into Sara-Kate's tiny eyes and felt the tiny eyes of elves upon her. Here she had watched Sara-Kate work coatless in the cold and learned about thick skins and private languages.

Hillary had only to crouch between the little houses to see Sara-Kate flick a strand of wheat-colored hair over her shoulder.

("It isn't where you look for elves so much as how you look," she would hear Sara-Kate say. "You can't just stomp around the place expecting to be shown things. Go slowly and quietly, and look deep.")

Look deep. Every day Hillary looked. If she had not yet seen an elf, if she still couldn't be sure of Sara-Kate, it must be because she was not looking deep enough, she decided. She redoubled her efforts, in the upstairs room, in the yard, on the streets of the town, in the whole world for that matter. There was no place safe from her watchfulness now, and no person either. She felt her eyes turning tiny, like Sara-Kate's. She felt herself turning shrewd.

Out in the Connollys' yard, she hovered protectively over the little well. Its bottlecap bucket was frozen in place, but come spring it would work again, she thought. The Ferris wheel had stayed upright on its metal rod. Every afternoon, Hillary walked to it and turned it with her mittened hand to make sure it still worked. It always did.

The elves' sunken pool looked more like a skating rink. Remembering the power rafts, Hillary leaned over and tried to see special marks of activity. Sometimes there were none, and a dark feeling would come upon her. But more often, strange scratchings appeared on the ice, or a mysterious circular clearing would show up in the snow nearby, and Hillary's heart would beat faster. She would glance toward the Ferris wheel and see again how it had glowed and spun on that extraordinary night, and hear the bird cry that had sounded when it seemed least possible. She would remember how Sara-Kate had trusted her and been betrayed, how she had revealed herself and been hurt, and how every single thing Sara-Kate had taught her about elves had turned out to be true about the thin girl herself. Then Hillary was sure that she had been in the presence of an elf, and that the village was a special, magic place.

"A place that's got to be saved," she told her mother one day, not long after another rumor had swept the street: a new family wanted to buy the Connolly house; a nice family with a dog and two children.

"Saved?" Mrs. Lenox asked with a frown.

"Moved," Hillary explained. "I'm going to move it into our yard. That way, when the Connollys' house is sold, the village will still be here in case anyone wants it again. A place like that shouldn't be allowed to fall apart. It needs to have someone taking care of it."

Mrs. Lenox shook her head in a despairing way.

"Well, I don't know. You'd have to put it somewhere out of sight and out of the way. Your father has the garden laid out so carefully. We wouldn't want the Ferris wheel sticking up in the middle, and those little huts would get caught in the mower if they were put on the lawn."

"Oh, no. They couldn't possibly go there," Hillary agreed. "How about behind the garage?"

"But that's not a place at all. It's full of rocks and briers."

Hillary nodded. "It'll be perfect," she said. "I was checking it over this afternoon. It looks so terrible that I guess I never thought of it before. It just goes to show."

"Goes to show what?" Mrs. Lenox asked, but Hillary had gone out the back door into the yard again, and there was no answer.

"It's getting rather dark out there, and cold!" Hillary's mother called to her, opening the storm door a crack so her voice would be heard. "I think you should come in now. Hillary! Where are you?"

Very odd, but there was still no answer, and Hillary seemed to have disappeared.